M01

MW01125411

Sage Gardens Cozy Mystery Series

Cindy Bell

Copyright © 2015 Cindy Bell

All rights reserved.

ISBN-13: 978-1511893473

ISBN-10: 1511893478

Table of Contents

Chapter One

The sparkling water of the lake gave Samantha the peace that she had been anticipating. Once in a while her mind would wander back to less pleasant times in her life. Occasionally a nightmare would wake her far earlier than the dawn. It was one of these mornings that had led her out to a table by the lake along with her cup of tea. She often spent an hour or so in the morning just gazing out at the water. No one was around this morning and it was a far cry from the busy lifestyle she had been accustomed to before she had retired.

Looking back, Samantha questioned why she had never allowed herself to slow down and just appreciate the fresh air that filled her lungs, or the sound of the birds chirping. As she sat back in her chair she smiled to herself. She had fought retirement tooth and nail. She wanted to keep working as a crime journalist. She wanted to still be on top of what was happening in the world. But when she had finally given in to the idea, she had found that retirement could be just as adventurous.

Moving into the retirement community, Sage Gardens, had made a huge difference in her life. Her neighbors were nice, if not a little quick to gossip. There were many social activities that she often took part in. Most of all, the view of the water was stunning. There was something fascinating about being tucked away in a beautiful environment. Sure, she felt a little disconnected from the rest of the world now and then, but on the flip side, she felt as if Sage Gardens had become her own little world away from the rest of the world. There certainly was no dearth of drama to be had, and the few friendships she had made were ones that she could rely on.

As she took another sip of her tea, she swept her eyes once more over the water. The unblemished surface greeted her, until she was startled by a lump near the water's edge. At first she thought it was a gnarled tree root emerging from the surface. When she leaned forward to take a closer look she could see that it was much larger than a tree root. It appeared to be made from cloth. She stood up and walked to the edge of the water. Upon closer inspection she realized that it was a backpack. The residents of Sage Gardens would often lose things. Many of the older residents were a little forgetful, and so it was not unusual to find purses or jackets laying around. But Samantha could not remember seeing anyone with a backpack.

Samantha reached for it, but as she did the slick grass beside the water threatened to make her lose her footing. She frowned and glanced around. There was an abandoned fishing pole nearly hidden in the tall grass. She grabbed it and tried to pull the bag closer with it. The pole was too weak to force the bag closer. She pulled it back and wound it beneath one of the straps of the backpack. This was enough to steer it to the very edge of the water.

Samantha leaned forward again and this time was able to pluck the bag out of the water. Once it was on the grass she looked at it for a moment. It was just a plain, dark blue backpack. Although there was nothing unusual about it, her curiosity was piqued. Who would have a backpack like this and why would it have ended up in the water? It might have been her investigative nature, but she had a burning need to know.

She unzipped the backpack and peered inside at the contents. She hoped to find some ID in it so she could return it to its owner. On the very top there was a ratty baseball cap with the emblem of a local sports team on it. She moved it aside to see what was underneath. There was what looked like a granola bar, a pair of socks and a flashlight. All of it seemed pretty normal to pack if someone was taking a hiking trip, or even camping. But when she brushed aside the socks to see if there might be a wallet to identify the owner she was greeted by a brick of what she could only assume was cocaine. The sight of it made her eyes widen. Not since her days as a crime journalist had she seen anything like it. Yet, there it was right in front of her in the middle of Sage Gardens. She couldn't think of a more unlikely place to find drugs. Maybe a little pot here and there, some of it medicinal, but nothing stronger than that.

Samantha was very nervous as she eyed the bag. Her first instinct was to get as far away from the bag as possible. But what if someone else came across it? She would feel terrible if someone else got into trouble because she had left it by the side of the water. The only thing she could think to do was get the bag to Eddy. Eddy was a retired detective, and she was sure that he would know what to do. When she picked up the bag water streamed out of it. She cringed and held it away from her clothes. She hoisted it up the gently sloping hill to her porch. She thought about taking it inside, but she didn't want the water dripping all over her floor. She set it down near the side door behind some plants to hide it and stepped inside. If whoever had lost the backpack was out looking for it, she didn't want it to be spotted with her. As soon as she was inside her villa she pulled out her cell phone and dialed Eddy's number.

"Oh, please answer, please have your phone on!" Samantha muttered. Eddy was known for having a cell phone, but very rarely actually turning it on. Luckily, on the fourth ring he answered.

"Hello?" Eddy's brusque voice carried clearly through the phone.

"Eddy, it's me, Samantha."

"I know that, I have caller ID," Eddy reminded her with some impatience.

"Listen, I don't have time for your antics. I need your help." Samantha felt the sense of urgency within her building with every moment that passed.

"What's wrong?" Eddy's concern was clear.

"I found something, and now I don't know what to do with it. Can you come over? Please?" Samantha clung to her phone tightly. It wasn't often that she asked for help, but in this case she felt she needed it. Being a retired detective she was sure Eddy would know what to do. Not only that, he was a take charge kind of guy who could handle a crisis well. She didn't want to mention anything over the phone as she had no idea who might overhear her.

"I'll be right there." Eddy knew it was unusual for Samantha to be so demanding. She was normally polite with a sunny personality that verged on irritating. He placed his gray fedora on his head, grabbed his jacket and headed straight out the door.

Cars were an afterthought in Sage Gardens as just about everything that the residents needed was within walking distance. If they wanted to go to the mall or somewhere further a bus was usually available to take them. Eddy didn't have to walk far to get to Samantha's villa. When he knocked on the door she opened it immediately as if she had been waiting on the other side.

"Come in!" Samantha grabbed his hand and

tugged him inside. Eddy was a little flustered. It wasn't often that she was so forceful.

"What's going on?" He frowned.

"I found something in the water." Samantha wrung her hands together and tried to calm down.

"It's not another dead duck, is it Samantha? I told you Simon will take care of that." He shook his head. "I'm not going near it."

"No, it isn't a dead duck." Samantha felt impatient as she glared at him. "It'll be easier if I just show you. Follow me." She turned towards the side door. With every step towards it she felt her blood pressure rise. She had no idea what she was going to do about the situation that she had gotten herself into.

Eddy followed her to the side door of the villa. She opened it and pointed to the tiled floor behind some plants where she had left the backpack. "You will not believe what's inside."

"Inside of what?" Eddy looked around with confusion. All he saw were some pot plants and

8

dead leaves.

Samantha turned to look as well. "Oh no! It's gone!" For a split second she was relieved, then the fear kicked in.

"What's gone? The duck?" Eddy was confused.

"Stop it about the duck! It's not a duck!" Samantha had desperation in her voice. "Eddy, it was drugs, hard drugs," her voice rose with her panic.

"Samantha!" Eddy grabbed her firmly by the elbow and steered her back inside the villa. "You can't be yelling about drugs out in the open like that. Do you want to get us both arrested?"

Samantha barely heard him. She felt dazed and a little numb. She wasn't sure if she had hallucinated the entire incident. If it were not for the small puddles on the tiled path where the bag had been she might have believed that none of it had happened.

"I was just sitting out by the water, when I saw

this backpack floating. I pulled it out. I thought maybe someone had lost it. But when I looked inside there were just a few normal things and then a brick of, well, I think it was cocaine. I mean, I don't know for sure, but that's what it looked like." She wiped sweat from her brow. She was so flustered that her heart was racing. "Now it's gone. But how is that possible? Where could it go?"

"That is a problem." Eddy swept his gaze over the hill and water by Samantha's villa. "It certainly didn't just get up and walk off. Which means that someone took it. If that someone decides it's lost and turns it into the police your fingerprints are going to be all over everything in it. Did you touch the drugs, Samantha?" He turned back to look at her. His expression was one she recognized. Eddy had a look that she called his 'cop look'. His jaw would tense, and his eyes would narrow just enough to get his point across.

"Of course not, I don't use drugs." Samantha looked at him with disgust. Not even in her youth had she touched anything that might alter her mental state. She was always very cautious to remain as alert as possible.

"I meant, did you touch them with your hands. Did you leave your prints on them?" Eddy frowned. "I'm not accusing you of anything, I just need to know the whole story."

"Oh well, I might have touched them, just to get a closer look." She closed her eyes as she realized the mistake she had made. "It's not like I expected the bag to be stolen."

"All right, then there is only one thing we can do." He reached into his pocket for his cell phone.

"What are you doing?" Samantha asked. She looked at him anxiously.

"Samantha, we have to call the police." Eddy frowned as he looked through the open side door at the puddle on the tiles. "The sooner we notify them, the better."

"No! We can't! What are we going to tell them?" Samantha asked incredulously. "Hello officer, I found some drugs, but then I lost them?" She looked at Eddy with frustration. "I called you here to help me, not get me arrested."

"It's better than that backpack turning up somewhere with your fingerprints all over it, Samantha," Eddy snapped out his words. When he saw the flinch of fear on Samantha's face he sighed. "I'm sorry, I don't mean to be harsh. But it's very important that you report this. I have connections at the department. No one is going to think that they were your drugs if you tell the truth now. If you don't, and the police find the backpack with your fingerprints, it will be less likely that they will believe you."

Samantha shook her head as a wave of panic washed over her. If only she had left that bag alone, maybe she wouldn't be in this situation. "If you really think it's the right thing to do, Eddy, I guess it's what we should do."

"I'll make the call." He dialed his phone and spoke quietly and quickly to the officer who picked up. He made sure that the responding officers would know that he was a retired detective. That still seemed to get him some leeway when it came to the police. Samantha felt her stomach churn. Her heart was pounding too loudly for her to be able to focus on what Eddy was saying. When he hung up the phone he looked over at her with sympathy. "You have to calm down, Samantha. If I were the detective looking into this I'd think you had bodies buried in the garden."

"Eddy! How is that supposed to help me calm down?" Samantha growled. She closed her eyes for a moment. She tried to visualize a peaceful sight to calm her, but she kept seeing that backpack instead.

"I'll get you a cup of tea." Eddy held open the side door for her. Samantha stepped inside and walked over to the couch. She sank down into it, as if the weight of the world was on her shoulders. Eddy fumbled his way through her kitchen to make her some tea. When the kettle whistled Eddy grabbed it without thinking. "Ouch!" he cussed under his breath.

"Eddy, are you okay?" Samantha asked.

"I'm fine, I'm fine, just relax." He poured her a cup of tea and carried it out to her. "Careful, it's hot."

Samantha nodded and took the tea from him. She began to blow on the surface of the tea lightly. As the steam drifted with the force of her breath, there was a knock on the front door. Samantha gulped down a mouthful of burning hot tea. She felt it singe all the way down her throat.

"I'll let them in," Eddy called out as he walked over to the door. Samantha thought about telling him to stop. But she knew it was too late. The police were already there. If they didn't answer the door they weren't just going to shrug and drive away.

Eddy opened the door. "Come in, come in." He stepped aside. Two officers made their way inside. Even though Samantha knew that Eddy was a retired detective, it was different having two active police officers in full uniform in her living room, especially since she had both found and lost quite a bit of drugs. The two officers looked almost identical with close-cropped, light brown hair and nearly matching brown eyes, but one of the officers was at least a foot taller than the other.

"You called in the report?" the taller officer asked Eddy.

"I did. But I'm not the one who found the backpack. She is." Eddy looked over at Samantha. She shifted from one foot to the other as the two officers focused their attention on her.

"Ma'am, where is the backpack?" the shorter officer asked.

"It's gone." Samantha frowned. She looked between the two officers anxiously.

"Gone?" the tall officer questioned. "What do you mean?"

Samantha took a deep breath. She knew that the best thing to do was tell the truth. "I pulled it out of the water, and took a look inside. When I saw the drugs I carried it up to my villa. I put it by the side door behind some plants, and when I went back to show Eddy it was gone."

"You're saying you left a backpack full of illegal drugs out in the open?" the short officer asked.

"They weren't my illegal drugs." Samantha felt her desperation rising. "The bag was in the water, it was all wet. I didn't want it dripping across my carpet."

"Why didn't you make the report right away instead of calling a friend?" the officer asked with some irritation.

"Well I, I just didn't know," Samantha stumbled over her words and then her voice trailed off. She looked at Eddy helplessly. Eddy offered her a sympathetic smile and turned towards the officers.

"She wanted to make sure that it was what she thought it was," Eddy said. "She didn't want to waste your time, if she was mistaken about what she had found. That's why she called me."

Samantha felt a sense of relief. She was very grateful that Eddy was there to help her deal with the situation. The shorter officer nodded and then looked over at Samantha again. "How long has the bag been missing?" he asked.

"About ten minutes," Samantha replied quickly. "Eddy called as soon as he saw that it was missing."

"So, you never actually saw the bag?" The taller officer made a note in his notebook and then looked up at Eddy.

"No, I didn't. But if Samantha said it was there, it was there." He nodded with confidence. Samantha was a little warmed by the gesture of support. "You can see where there is some water on the tiles from the bag dripping."

The officers exchanged a long look, then the taller of the two spoke again. "We'll take a look around. Without the backpack there's not much that we can do." The officer nodded at Samantha and Eddy. As Samantha watched the two officers walk out through the side door, she felt foolish.

"What they must think of me," she muttered. Her cheeks were flushed with embarrassment.

"They don't think anything about you other than that you are a concerned citizen." Eddy watched the officers as they walked down to the water where Samantha had found the backpack in the first place. "Let's see if they find anything."

Eddy held the door for her and Samantha stepped out. They trailed after the police officers, leaving enough space that they wouldn't interfere with the investigation. From what Samantha could see it wasn't much of one. The officers stood at the water for a few minutes. They spoke casually to one another. The shorter officer peered over his shoulder back up at the side door of Samantha's villa. Then he looked back out over the water again.

"Do they think it's going to jump up out of the water like a fish?" Samantha asked.

"They're probably checking to see if someone tossed it back into the water," Eddy suggested. He tucked his hands deep into the pockets of his trousers. His lips set with displeasure as he watched the two officers turn around and walk back towards them. They hadn't even walked the entire lake.

"Nothing there." The short officer pursed his lips. "So, I guess, if you find it again, hang onto it this time and give us a call."

"That's it?" Samantha asked. She looked between the officers with surprise.

"Well, like I said, not much we can do with no evidence, no crime." The taller officer shrugged. "We have your report, and if you notice anything out of the ordinary be sure to let us know. We'll take one more walk down by the water on our way out."

"Thanks," Samantha said feeling embarrassed. Not only had she found and lost a bag full of drugs, she had also wasted the officers' time for absolutely nothing. It seemed to her that if she had just slept in, all of the drama could have been avoided.

"We'll be in touch." Eddy nodded at the two

officers. Inwardly, he was considering calling in a report on both of them. They had barely evaluated the situation and didn't have a very helpful demeanor. They hadn't even bothered to identify themselves. But he recalled that when he was a young officer he had a bit of an attitude as well. Something about the badge and the gun could make a young man arrogant.

"I'm sorry, Eddy. I don't know what I was thinking." Samantha shook her head.

"You didn't do anything wrong, Samantha. You were just trying to help. Why don't we take a look around together?" Eddy gestured to the tiled area. "We can start where you left the bag. If someone snatched it, they must have been on foot. Maybe there's something that the officers overlooked."

"I think that is a definite possibility," Samantha mumbled. While looking along the side of the villa Samantha noticed that there was a smudge of mud on one of the tiles. She had just cleaned it, and she knew that she hadn't tracked anything onto the tiles. It looked like half of a footprint. "Look at this, Eddy!" She pointed it out to him.

Eddy walked over to her and looked down at it. "Where there's mud, if someone has been here, there's going to be a footprint in the mud nearby." He began scanning the area surrounding the side door for any evidence of a footprint. It didn't take him long to discover that there was one just beside the bushes that shielded Samantha's side window. "Here it is!" He peered closely at the impression in the mud. Samantha stepped up behind him.

"Do you think it is from whoever took the bag?" She studied the footprint as well.

"I think it probably is. It rained early this morning, so this must have happened between that time and now. I don't think too many people would have been lurking around the side window. Can you get a picture of it with your phone? It might be a good way for us to find matching prints. We might be able to figure out at least in which direction they went."

"Do you think that it could be one of the officer's shoes?" Samantha suggested. She aimed the camera on her phone towards the footprint.

"No, I don't think so. The pattern of the sole looks more like the pattern you would find on the bottom of tennis shoes. Don't you think?" He pointed to the ridges in the soil. Samantha nodded and took a close-up picture of the footprint.

"Well, we found one. Now, we just have to see if we can find anymore," she suggested.

"Let's look more towards the water. The ground is softer there, and my guess would be that whoever it was approached from that direction."

Eddy and Samantha began scouring the grass and mud that led down to the water. As Samantha inched her way towards the edge of the water the wind rustled the tall grass that surrounded it. As they walked in silence Samantha's mind raced. She still couldn't believe that she had lost the backpack. It had only been a few minutes between the time she set it down, and the time she went back to look for it. Had the person who took the backpack been watching her the entire time? One thing was for sure, whoever it was knew where she lived.

"I don't see anything." Samantha shook her head as she continued to look at the ground.

"All it takes is one footprint." Eddy kept his eyes locked to the ground.

"That's true." Samantha had to look up. Her neck was starting to ache. She turned to look at the officers who were still down by the water. She could see from where she stood that their shoes were definitely not tennis shoes. As she watched the two officers suddenly hunched down. One whipped out his radio while the other pulled back the tall grass.

"Eddy, I think they found something," Samantha said as she watched one of the officers run up the hill to the parked patrol car.

"It must be something bad. Police officers don't move that fast over a backpack." Eddy grimaced. "Let's go take a closer look."

Samantha nodded and followed after him down the slope of the grass towards the edge of the water. The shorter officer was still hunched down beside the tall grass. When he heard them approaching he whirled around with his gun drawn.

"Hey, calm down!" Eddy demanded. He positioned himself between the gun and Samantha. Samantha's breath caught in her chest.

"You both need to step back." The officer slowly lowered his gun.

"Yes, officer," Samantha replied. She moved back slowly. When the second officer returned he had a small medical bag.

"Clear the way," he commanded as he brushed past Samantha and Eddy. The tall grass parted as the officer pushed through it. Eddy took a sharp breath as he saw what was beyond it.

"Don't look, Samantha!" Eddy moved between her and the tall grass. "Trust me."

Samantha frowned. She knew that she could

handle the sight of whatever Eddy was hiding, but she didn't want to upset him by forcing the issue. She was certain that she would find out soon enough.

"Who is it?" she asked.

"The bus driver." Eddy frowned. "It looks like he was murdered."

Chapter Two

"Oh no!" Samantha gasped in shock at the realization that the bus driver was dead.

The driver of the activities bus was at Sage Gardens nearly every day. He was a nice enough man. Samantha hadn't really gotten to know him very well. She didn't often participate in the activities as she preferred to drive on her own wherever she pleased.

"We should give them some space." Eddy took her gently by the elbow and steered her away from the grass. Samantha was still a little stunned. The morning had started out in the strangest way, and now before noon it had become tragic. She wasn't sure what to think about the possible connection between the backpack and the body.

They had both been near the water. Was it possible that the backpack had belonged to Vince, the driver? If it didn't belong to Vince then could it possibly belong to the killer? Could the killer have taken it from outside her door?

"I see that brain spinning." Eddy gave her elbow a gentle squeeze. "What is it?"

"I was just wondering if there might be a connection between the backpack I found and Vince being murdered." Samantha frowned as she looked back at the flurry of activity by the water. More officers had arrived as well as the coroner's van.

"It could be a coincidence." Eddy narrowed his eyes. "But I think it's unlikely. Would you excuse me a moment, Samantha?"

"Sure." Samantha nodded and followed his gaze up the hill towards the parking lot. A man was climbing out of a white SUV. Eddy headed straight for the SUV. Samantha took another step back and watched what was unfolding around her. The officers had the crime scene cordoned off.

Samantha noticed a few of the residents of Sage Gardens poking their heads out of their villas to see what was happening. She knew that the murder would be all anyone would talk about.

Since Samantha was involved, she would be battered with questions the moment they could get her alone. Samantha didn't care about that. She cared about the young man who was now dead. Had he been there in the grass when she was drinking her tea that morning? She felt awful at the idea. She had been enjoying the view and trying to relax, all the time not knowing that someone had been murdered only a few feet away. She shivered and started to walk back towards her villa.

"Samantha, wait," Eddy called out to her as he made his way down the hill. The man from the SUV was trailing right behind him. Samantha squinted against the mid-morning sun as the man drew closer.

"Samantha, this is Detective Brunner, he's running the investigation into the murder." Eddy gestured towards the younger man who was searching through his cell phone.

"Pleasure to meet you, Detective Brunner." Samantha waited for the man to look up, but he did not.

"I thought Detective Brunner might want to speak with you since you are the one who found the bag," Eddy explained.

"Of course," Samantha replied with some hesitation. She wasn't sure if she wanted to speak to the detective. After all, she hadn't seen anyone. She had only fished out a backpack. She wasn't sure what good that could do the investigation. Yet again she would have to face her own foolishness when she admitted that she had let the backpack go missing in order to protect her carpets.

"Now, you say that you were down by the water when you spotted the backpack." Detective Brunner did not look up from his phone.

"That's right." Samantha nodded. "I was having a cup of tea."

"You noticed the backpack in the water, and you thought you should get it out, is that right?" Detective Brunner tapped lightly on the screen of his phone. Samantha didn't think it was very polite not to even look in her direction, but she also knew that Detective Brunner was a busy man and he was focused on the crime, which was important. He was likely perusing photographs of suspects, or close ups of the crime scene.

"Well, I figured it must belong to someone. I thought maybe someone had left it behind and somehow it got pushed into the water." She wondered if it would have been better if she had left the backpack in the water. Maybe no one else would have found it. What did it matter that she had found it? It was gone now, and she was stuck answering questions.

"I see." He jerked his hand with the cell phone in it. Then he grunted. "Lost again," he muttered. When he tucked his phone into his pocket Samantha caught a glimpse of the screen. He had been playing some kind of game. Her eyes widened at the sight. She glanced over at Eddy but he didn't seem to notice.

"Maybe the backpack was with the body?" Eddy swept his gaze over the tall grass. "Maybe the body washed up in the grass."

"No, it looks like he was murdered where we found his body." Detective Brunner glanced over his shoulder. "The body was hidden by the grass. If we hadn't been looking for the backpack it probably would have taken a few days before the body was found. It makes me think that whoever did this didn't have time to move the body or was planning on getting out of town pretty fast."

"How terrible." Samantha shook her head. "He was a nice man."

"Did you know him well?" Detective Brunner looked at her with interest.

Samantha felt a pang of guilt as she thought about whether she should have taken the time to get to know Vince better. He was the type that would crack a joke and always seemed to be laughing. She hadn't really made the effort to talk to him. She felt like she had tried her best to connect with people at Sage Gardens, but had found that she was rejected by the social butterflies that ran all of the events. She had settled into a strange but satisfying friendship with Eddy and a few others. That was enough for her.

"No, I didn't know him well. I just saw him come and go. He was the driver for the activities bus," she explained. "I don't think I have ever even had a conversation with him."

"Then what made you think he was nice?" Detective Brunner asked.

"He was courteous. He would help his passengers up the steps if they needed it. He always said hello to the office staff. Any time I saw him he was smiling or laughing," Samantha said as she looked back over at the grass. "I can't understand why anyone would want to kill him."

"Maybe for the backpack full of drugs?" Detective Brunner spoke in a dry tone.

Samantha narrowed her eyes and pursed her lips. She felt as if Detective Brunner was making fun of her.

"If she remembers anything else, I'll let you

know." Eddy offered his hand to Detective Brunner. Detective Brunner gave it a quick shake. Then he began walking over to the crime scene.

"He's a new detective," Eddy muttered, as if that explained the detective's behavior. "He's still getting his feet wet."

"Eddy, I know that he is a detective, but I don't think he's taking this case very seriously." Samantha frowned with concern. She didn't think it was appropriate at all that he was playing a game during an investigation.

"You have to understand, Sam, that detectives see these types of crimes all the time. Just because it may not seem like he's focused on the case, doesn't mean that he isn't. It's just that finding a dead body isn't as shocking to them after seeing so many." Eddy shrugged. "I'm sure he'll do a fine job."

"I think that it should be shocking every time," Samantha said heatedly as she watched the body bag being loaded into the back of the coroner's van. "He was somebody. He deserves a thorough investigation into his murder."

"You're right. I'll keep an eye on him. If he's not up to snuff then I'll look into it further. All right?" He placed a hand lightly on the curve of Samantha's shoulder. Samantha relaxed a little at the touch. Despite how tough and standoffish Eddy could be, he often knew the right moment to be tender.

"I think that we need to find out some things for ourselves, too. I mean the backpack is still missing. Plus we found that footprint." Samantha started to walk back up the hill. "We should see if we can pick up the trail."

"Samantha." Eddy followed after her. "This really isn't the kind of case to get into the middle of. I mean we have no idea who this man was. Maybe this happened because of criminal activity. Maybe someone was getting revenge. It's best to let the authorities look into it."

"Oh, I'll let them all right. But the moment that they don't follow through, I'll be looking into things for myself." Samantha's eyes narrowed with determination. She felt that there was more to the murder than the police would assume. Something just did not feel right about it.

"I bet you will." Eddy offered her a tolerant smile. "Why don't we go have that tea that you missed out on? We should let Walt know what happened. You know he doesn't handle surprises well."

"Good idea." Samantha looked towards Walt's villa with concern. As a retired accountant Walt liked things to be a certain way, and finding a body in the grass near his home was sure to make him uneasy. As they walked towards Walt's villa, Samantha couldn't help looking back at the crime scene. She saw that the police had roped off a good portion of it, but she thought that they should have roped off more. Everyone who lived in Sage Gardens was at least a little nosy. The police could lose a lot of evidence if residents began trampling so close to the crime scene. "I just want to take one more quick look at the crime scene. Okay?"

Eddy tried not to smile at her. She had the

mind of a cop whether she wanted to admit it or not, and he admired her for it, whether he liked to admit it or not. He nodded. "A quick look."

The two walked back over to the roped off area. Samantha was careful to give the crime scene a wide berth. She crouched down and looked towards the tall grass. "How was he positioned, Eddy?"

"His head was towards the water." Eddy glanced over the blood stained grass. "It looked like he had fallen backwards."

"So, the attacker probably came from up the hill." Samantha looked up towards the hill. "But that doesn't make much sense."

"Why not?" Eddy asked.

Samantha stood up and turned to face the hill. "If I was standing here, I could see anyone who was coming."

"That's true." Eddy looked up the hill and then back down at the water. "If I saw someone who I was afraid of, I certainly would not have run towards the water."

"So, it's possible that the killer is someone that Vince knew." Samantha smiled.

"Good eye, Samantha." Eddy was about to turn away from the crime scene when he noticed something just beyond the yellow tape. There was another indentation in the soil. He leaned closer. "Samantha, get your phone out. I think we've found another footprint."

Samantha pulled out her cell phone and aimed it where Eddy pointed. The footprint was not as well defined, but it was there. The imprint seemed similar to the other footprint, but it was difficult to tell for sure.

"Got it," she said confidently.

"Great. Can you send those pictures to me?" he asked hopefully as he wasn't quite sure how that worked.

"No problem. They should be in your e-mail in a few minutes."

"Thanks. Maybe we can get a good enough

image to make a match if we make the pictures larger. Let's head over to Walt's and see what he thinks of all of this."

Eddy began walking up the hill. Samantha followed after him. As she climbed the hill she imagined what it would have been like to see her killer looking down at her. Did Vince know him? Did Vince call out his name? Was he happy to see him? She shuddered at the thought.

Chapter Three

Walt was already on his porch when Eddy and Samantha walked up to his villa.

"What's going on?" Walt looked anxious as he gripped the railing of the porch. "I saw the police cars taking off."

"We're here to tell you. But maybe we should go inside?" Eddy nodded towards Samantha. "Samantha needs something for her nerves."

"I'm fine, Eddy." Samantha shot him a stubborn look.

"Sure you are." He gestured for all of them to step inside. Walt held the door for Samantha. Once they were inside he set a pot of tea on the stove to brew.

"It must be something bad. It's something bad isn't it?" Walt frowned. He ran his fingertips along the tea bags to make sure that they were all evenly placed inside the box.

"The police found the body of the activities

bus driver in the grass by the water," Eddy explained.

"Vince, wasn't it?" Walt asked. "How terrible. He seemed like a good person."

"Did you ever talk to him?" Samantha asked.

"Not really. You know I can't stand the idea of getting on one of those buses." He cringed at the very idea. "They are very unsafe, and impossible to keep clean." He poured tea for each of them and set the cups down on napkins on the table. "How did he die?"

"It looks like he was stabbed," Eddy's voice lowered slightly. Samantha was suddenly glad that Eddy hadn't allowed her to take a closer look. From his expression she could tell that it was a gory sight.

"How terrible," Walt repeated. "This is going to get all of the residents pretty upset."

"So, none of us really knew him?" Samantha added. "It seems sad, doesn't it? That someone can be a regular part of your life without you ever getting to know them?"

"Well, it's a bit like the gardener I suppose." Walt shrugged.

"I actually know Simon pretty well." Samantha smiled. "He always gives me tips for my little garden."

"Simon is very friendly." Eddy nodded his head in agreement.

"Well, I didn't mean this gardener, but I mean when we are in our daily routine it is easy to overlook the people that only play a small role," he said. "If that makes sense."

"I guess." Samantha nodded a little. "I just wish I hadn't let the backpack out of my sight."

"Backpack?" Walt questioned.

"Samantha found a backpack in the river before the body was found," Eddy explained. "It had drugs in it, cocaine. But when she brought it up to her villa she left it outside, because it was wet, and a few minutes later when she took me to see it, it was missing."

"Wow!" Walt said with wide eyes. "I wonder who took it. You need to be very careful, Sam."

"I will be." She nodded. "I still think that it's important that we find out what really happened to Vince. I have a feeling that the police will be eager to dismiss the murder as quickly as they discovered it."

"What makes you think that?" Eddy asked. He spoke with a bit of defensiveness in his voice.

"I think it will be easy to just assume that Vince's death was drug related, rather than looking into it thoroughly. I don't mean that they won't do their job, Eddy. I just think they'll try to solve the murder as quickly as possible. I doubt that they will consider Vince an important person," she said grimacing. "It's not right, but it's the truth, isn't it?"

"Not always. You have to have a little more faith in the police, Samantha. Let's give them their chance to investigate and see what they turn up. Like I said before, if I don't think they're doing a good job of it, then we'll decide if we want to get involved. All right?" He looked at Samantha, hoping that she would agree.

Samantha was silent as she stared down at the table. Walt stood up and began to clear the tea cups from the table.

"Eddy is right, we need to let this rest for now, Samantha," Walt said sternly, but his gaze was gentle. "There's no need to get in the middle of things when we don't know any more information than the police do. I mean, what could we possibly find out that they couldn't?" He carried the cups over to the sink and set them carefully inside.

"I'm not sure. But I just feel like we need to try." Samantha frowned. She fidgeted with the napkin that had been under her cup.

"I think you feel a little guilty," Eddy suggested. He looked at her with a hesitant smile. "It's not your fault, Samantha. You know that, don't you?"

"Why would she feel guilty?" Walt asked. He looked very confused as he carefully washed the tea cups.

"Because, she didn't hear or see anything. Samantha, I'm sure the murder took place before you ever even woke up this morning. How could you know?" He met her eyes directly. "There was nothing that you could have done."

Samantha nodded a little, but she didn't really agree. If she had slept with her window open she might have heard screams or an argument. If she had gotten up to use the bathroom, she might have noticed someone running past her window. Instead, she had been oblivious to the fact that someone was being murdered just outside. It seemed impossible to her that she had gone about her morning, making tea, walking down to the water, without ever sensing that something wasn't right.

"There was nothing you could have done," Walt repeated Eddy's words. "What happened wasn't good, but you know, it seems like Vince made his own bed."

"What does that mean?" Samantha asked. She looked at Walt intently.

"I mean, he was probably involved in drug dealing. That's not exactly good for your health." Walt sat back down at the table.

"Walt, I didn't expect you to be like that." Samantha frowned with distaste.

"Like what? Statistically speaking those that engage in criminal behavior run a much higher chance of meeting an untimely death. It's just math." He looked up at Samantha with a puzzled expression. "Did I say something upsetting?"

"I think that Samantha just means that Vince is not a statistic, he's someone we all knew," Eddy explained.

"Samantha, I didn't mean to offend you." Walt looked at her with concern.

"You didn't, Walt, it's okay. I think this entire experience is catching up with me." She stood up from the table. "I'm going to head home. It's been a long morning for me," Samantha muttered. She was still annoyed with Walt. He was brilliant, but sometimes his intelligence seemed to limit his empathy. Eddy watched as she walked out of the villa. Samantha's shoulders were slumped with the weight of the burden that she was carrying.

As Samantha walked towards her villa, she noticed some commotion near the office. There was a police car, as well as two officers talking to the gardener. Samantha stared as the two officers stepped closer to the gardener. Simon was a gentle giant, well over six foot and with a forehead as broad as a billboard. He didn't talk much, but he worked hard at keeping the grounds tended. She couldn't imagine what business the officers would have with him.

"If you're going to stare, you might as well get closer." Eddy stepped up from just behind her.

"Eddy, what have I told you about sneaking up on me?" Samantha shot him an annoyed look.

"It's not my fault that your observational skills have become rusty over the years." Eddy smirked.

"Oh trust me, there's nothing rusty about my observational skills. But I've become accustomed to people not popping up out of nowhere." She looked back at the officers in time to see them handcuffing Simon. "What are they doing?"

"Looks like they have a suspect in mind," Eddy's voice grew grim. He didn't look any more convinced than Samantha was. "Maybe, we should find out before they drive off."

"That's ridiculous!" Samantha frowned as she watched the officers restrain Simon. "Simon would never hurt anyone. You're right, let's go see what's going on."

Samantha and Eddy walked towards the police officers. Simon was barely holding back tears. "But I didn't do anything. I didn't do anything," he kept repeating. Samantha could hear the tears in his voice. Her heart ached for him as she knew that he had to be terrified. "I don't know how it got in there, honestly I don't."

"We'll figure that out when we get downtown," the officer said sternly. He steered Simon towards the police car. The problem was he was quite large and his hands were cuffed so it was difficult to get him into the backseat of the patrol car.

"What's the meaning of this?" Samantha demanded. She walked right up to the officers.

"Samantha," Eddy chastised. But it was too late. The officers had just managed to get Simon into the backseat. They both turned to face Samantha with irritated expressions.

"Is there a problem?" the taller officer asked.

"Why are you taking this man into custody?" Samantha demanded. Her tone was verging on disrespectful.

"He's in custody because he's suspected of murder." The officer looked between Eddy and Samantha. His demeanor shifted from annoyed to stern. "Is there something that you know, that we don't?"

"Just that Simon is not a killer," Samantha said with clear confidence. She had a tendency to be very protective. She had seen a lot of injustice during her time as a crime journalist. Just because a person was convicted of a crime, that didn't always mean that they were guilty of that crime. She didn't want to see Simon go through that, too. Although, she didn't like to cross the police, she would if she thought someone was being wrongfully accused.

"Oh? How do you know that?" The officer took a step closer to Samantha.

"I just do. He's a good man. He keeps to himself." Samantha straightened her shoulders and planted her feet firmly. She was determined not to be intimidated.

"So, he puts on a good show and remains isolated?" The officer shook his head. "Classic psychopathic behavior."

"Someone's been watching too many crime shows," Eddy muttered under his breath. He could feel the tension building between the officer and Samantha. He knew that it was only a matter of time before she blew and that could lead to her being in handcuffs. "Look, what possible proof could you have that Simon is the killer?"

"Although, you are not someone I have to

prove anything to, if you must know, we found the murder weapon in his toolbox." The officer gestured to an open metal toolbox on the ground beside him. "Now, do you have anything else that you would like to add?"

Samantha watched as the other officer bagged the bloody screwdriver for evidence. Her stomach flipped anxiously. If it was true that Simon had the murder weapon, the case against him would be a slam dunk. She wondered if it was possible that she could have been so off base about him.

"So, he was just walking around with the murder weapon in his toolbox?" Eddy said with disbelief. "That doesn't make much sense to me."

"Murder doesn't make much sense to me." The officer narrowed his eyes. "So, I don't expect killers to make sense either."

"Good point," Eddy agreed. He glanced over at Samantha. She was still staring at the bagged murder weapon.

"Here is my card." The officer handed over a business card to each of them. "If either of you think of anything that you feel has something to do with this case, please feel free to call."

Samantha clutched the card tightly. She nodded as the officer walked over to the car.

"Strange case," Eddy's quiet words trailed after the car as it drove out of Sage Gardens.

"I just find it very hard to believe, Eddy. Of all the people I have met since I have moved to Sage Gardens, Simon would be one of the last that I would consider dangerous."

"I have to say he's never struck me as someone to watch out for, even with his size. He's always been friendly enough to me," Eddy retorted with a puzzled frown. "But with the murder weapon in his toolbox, it's hard to question the arrest."

"Why would he hide it in his toolbox?" Samantha questioned. "Wouldn't he just get rid of it?"

"Maybe he panicked," Eddy said. "Didn't think it through."

"I guess it's possible," Samantha said but she wasn't convinced.

"Let me walk you back to your villa." Eddy smiled sympathetically at her. "I want to make sure you get some rest."

"How could I rest knowing that Simon has been arrested for something that he didn't do?" She shook her head. "No, I won't be resting. Not until Simon is out of jail."

"I think you're taking this far too seriously, Samantha. It's not as if they're going to hang him by his toes and torture him. They'll question him. With the murder weapon in his possession they might book him, but if he's innocent they'll uncover the truth. Simon will be fine." Eddy began to lead her back towards her villa.

"Will he, Eddy?" Samantha asked. "Have you ever thought about how traumatic it is for a person to be wrongly accused and held against their will?"

"It's not exactly the same thing as being taken hostage," Eddy pointed out in a grim tone. They paused outside Samantha's villa.

"Isn't it? I think it's exactly like it. If two armed men walked up to me, tied my hands and threw me in the backseat of their car, wouldn't that be an abduction?" She met his eyes with growing irritation. "How can you not see that?"

"I don't see that because the two men that have taken Simon into custody are not criminals, they are well trained officers of the law. They are sanctioned by the government of this country to be able to make decisions in order to keep the citizens of this country safe. Really, Samantha, sometimes I wonder if you're hoping for complete anarchy." He frowned and met her eyes with his own flashing gaze. "Get some rest."

With that he spun on his heel and stomped away. Samantha stared after him, just as flustered. Whenever she and Eddy discussed politics or police it did not go well. Samantha bit her tongue to keep from saying a few more words about what she thought of his opinion. She knew better. Once Eddy was done with a conversation he was done.

Chapter Four

Once inside her villa Samantha hoped to be able to relax. But she felt uneasy. The tea cup she had left behind when the police arrived was still waiting for her. She picked it up and dumped the contents into the sink. She had planned to drive into town for some groceries. She was going to stop off in a little thrift shop to look for something to brighten up the hallway. It was hard to simply continue with her day after such a jarring experience. She knew she couldn't go shopping, her mind was filled with blood and drugs. She wasn't sure if she would be able to rest. All she could think about was Simon and how scared he probably was.

Samantha was not someone that assumed everyone was innocent. In fact more than once she had proven someone was guilty of something. She often felt a bit of frustration towards the people around a perpetrator who acted as if he or she was innocent even though the evidence obviously indicated otherwise. However, when it came to Simon there was no question in her mind. She didn't think he had anything to do with the murder. The only problem was the pesky issue of the murder weapon being found in Simon's toolbox. It struck Samantha as a little strange that he even had a screwdriver, but she assumed some of the tools he used, such as the leaf blower, might require it for repair, or for when he hung up flower pots for the residents. So, had someone taken it out of his toolbox? Why would someone go to the trouble of breaking into the garden shed just to get a screwdriver?

Nothing about the murder made sense, right down to the body being found in the tall grass. Why had the murderer left his body in such an easy place to find? It might have taken longer if the police weren't looking for the drugs, but it still wasn't a place to leave a dead body. It led her to think that the crime might have been one of passion. Perhaps the murderer hadn't planned anything and had instead just become enraged.

Maybe in a panic the murderer had simply abandoned Vince's body. If that were the case then hopefully it wouldn't take long to figure out who had actually committed the crime.

Samantha shook her head in an attempt to clear her thoughts and began preparing a late lunch. She needed a chance to clear her mind, and sleep wasn't going to do that. On a whim she decided to call her friend, Jo. She could fill her in on the crime that had taken place, and have a sounding board for her frustrations with Eddy. When she called Jo, she almost didn't expect her to answer. Although Samantha considered Jo a friend, the jury was still out on Jo's opinion about her. Jo was a hard woman to get to know, and a harder woman to befriend. To Samantha's surprise, she did answer.

"Hi Sam. I was wondering when you would get around to calling me."

"What do you mean?" Samantha asked.

"I heard about the murder. I knew you'd be calling to fill me in sooner or later." She laughed a little. Samantha was relieved to hear that she was in a fairly good mood.

"I was wondering if you'd like to join me for lunch." Samantha gripped the phone tensely. She hoped she wasn't making a mistake by having Jo over. Although Samantha had a lot of respect for the woman, her friends, Walt and Eddy, didn't always share the same opinion. They were more interested in Jo's past than the present.

"I'd love to. I'll bring some wine!" Jo hung up before Samantha could argue about the wine. The truth was Samantha could really use a glass. She put together a salad to go along with some chicken for lunch. Within a few minutes Jo knocked on the door.

"Come on in!" Samantha called. She carried the food from the kitchen to the dining room table. Jo opened the door and stepped inside. Samantha was always a little dazzled by the sight of Jo. While Samantha had more of a simple beauty, Jo's looks were quite exotic. Between her olive skin and her thick, black hair she looked as if she could have walked right off a runway, even though she was in her sixties just like Samantha was. While Samantha's copper-red hair had a smattering of gray in it, Jo's was pure black. While Samantha's bright green eyes were crinkled by smile lines, Jo's face still had a youthful tautness to it. The woman was in immaculate shape as well. Despite her younger looks, it only took one look into her dark, haunted eyes to make her seem much older.

"Hi Sam." Jo placed the wine on the table and smiled at Samantha. "So, are you ready to give me the details? Did you solve the crime yet?"

"Not even close," Samantha said shaking her head. She walked back into the kitchen to get two wine glasses. When she returned, Jo had already opened the wine. She poured glasses for both of them. "The only thing I know for sure is that the police have arrested the wrong man."

"Oh really?" Jo raised an eyebrow. "Are you championing the underdog, yet again?"

Samantha took a sip of her wine. "I guess you

could say that. But I know I'm right. They arrested the gardener, Simon."

"He seems harmless." Jo frowned and sipped her own wine. "Why did they arrest him?"

"He had the murder weapon." Samantha cringed.

"Well, that's a pretty good reason. But it certainly doesn't make him guilty. How did you find out why they arrested him?" Jo eyed her curiously.

"It's a very long story." Samantha sighed and closed her eyes a moment. "Have some lunch."

Jo began eating her salad. She was still watching Samantha when Samantha opened her eyes again.

"So?" Jo prompted.

"So, I found this backpack filled with drugs..." Samantha began.

"Wait, what?" Jo set down her fork. "What kind of drugs?"

"Cocaine, I think. I don't know for sure

because before I could turn it over to the police it disappeared. When I left it outside because the bag was wet someone took it." Samantha took a bite of her salad.

"Samantha, this isn't good. You shouldn't be involved in any of this." Jo frowned. Her voice was heavy with concern. "Does anyone else know that it was you that found the backpack?"

"Only the police and Walt. I suppose it might have gotten around Sage Gardens, but I'm not sure. I think the news of the murder probably swept away any rumors about a backpack. Oh, and Eddy, of course," she added as an afterthought.

"Of course." Jo's eyes narrowed a bit. "Well, I think you should be very careful about who you tell, Samantha. You really should stay out of this. Understand?" She met Samantha's eyes across their glasses of wine.

"Yes, I do. But why?" Samantha frowned.

"Trust me, Samantha, getting involved would be the worst thing that you could do now." She took the last bite of her salad. "Be glad that someone took the backpack."

"But, what about Simon?" Samantha asked. "Am I supposed to just let him rot in jail?"

"He wouldn't be the first, and he won't be the last, besides I'm sure the police will discover the truth." Jo finished her wine. "This is not a crusade you should make your own, Samantha. It's too dangerous when drugs are involved. Don't say I didn't warn you. Thanks for lunch."

She stood up from the table. Samantha looked up at her with a mixture of confusion and a hint of anger. She had expected Jo of all people to understand. Jail was a horrible place for an innocent person. But then Jo hadn't exactly been innocent. She had been an infamous cat burglar that had given the police the run around for many years. Maybe that was why she didn't feel sympathy for Simon.

"You're welcome," Samantha finally spoke very quietly. She didn't stand up from the table. She didn't show Jo to the door. She felt as if all of the wind had faded from her sails.

"Remember what I said, Sam," Jo said. She stepped out the door and closed it behind her.

Alone once more Samantha wondered if her friends were right. Should she stay out of it? Her stubborn nature told her not to. But her stubborn nature had gotten her into plenty of messes before. Samantha finished her lunch and then sprawled out on the couch. She decided to take Eddy's advice and at least try to rest a little. She yawned as she stretched out. When she closed her eyes she saw an image of the backpack floating in the water.

Chapter Five

Samantha woke up to her phone ringing. She shifted uncomfortably on the couch. She had finally fallen asleep in an awkward position and it was difficult for her to sit up at first. She fumbled on the coffee table for her cell phone. As she answered she didn't even take the time to check the caller ID.

"Hello?" she mumbled.

"Samantha, I need you to come over."

"Who is this?" Samantha asked groggily. She blinked a few times to try to get her mind to focus.

"It's Eddy," he sounded a little insulted.

"Oh sorry, Eddy, I was napping. What did you need?" She wiped her hand across her eyes and yawned.

"I need you to come over. I want to show you something."

"Okay, I'll be there in a few minutes."

Samantha hung up the phone. She felt fairly groggy still. "That wine must have really done its work." She shook her head and stood up. As she got her balance she wondered what Eddy might have to show her. She was sure it was about the case. She grabbed her purse and slid her shoes on. She was out the door before she could even think about the state of her hair or her wrinkled clothing. She realized that she must have slept for a few solid hours as the sun was beginning to set.

In the twilight, Samantha noticed that there weren't any other residents of Sage Gardens out walking around. Normally in the warmer weather there were people everywhere on the grounds. It seemed as if they had all been scared off by the news of the murder. Even with a man in custody they were being more cautious. Samantha understood why. It was easy to feel vulnerable when age had begun to limit your ability to defend yourself.

Samantha often found herself off balance when she used to have very sure footing. As she walked towards Eddy's villa, she heard a splash in the water near her. Her stomach tightened. Just the reminder that the water was there was enough to bring back all the stress of the morning. She had been able to sleep away some of her thoughts about the murder, but now they all came flooding back. She remembered Jo's warning about what she was getting herself involved in. Samantha frowned and quickened her pace towards Eddy's villa.

As Samantha walked, she heard yet another splash. She shuddered at the sound. Her feet grew heavy, preventing her from walking much further. A crazy thought occurred to her. Could it be Vince trying to get her attention from the grave? She turned uneasily to look in the direction of the water. The tall grass rippled in the wind. Bold yellow crime-scene tape whipped and wobbled around the spot where Vince had been killed. That was not where the sound of the splashing was coming from.

As she stared, she heard another splash. She

turned towards the sound. It was further along the water's edge, in the opposite direction of Eddy's villa. She knew that she should just continue towards his villa, but her curiosity was now piqued. Not only that but she had a tendency to want to confront anything that made her afraid. Her father had told her when she was just a little girl, that things aren't so scary once you stand up to them. So, she had always done her best to stand up to whatever frightened her.

Without really deciding to, she began to walk in the direction of the splashing sound. It sounded much too small to be a fish. It sounded as if someone was tossing something into the water. Sage Gardens did allow fishing in the lake, however it was not the season for it just yet. A few of the residents had been known to toss in a line even when they were not supposed to. Samantha guessed that might be what she was hearing. But she still wanted to see for herself.

As she slowly approached the area of the shore that she had heard the sound coming from, she noticed a man reclining in a chair. He looked quite comfortable. He held one hand in a loose fist. The other was poised in the air, about to throw something. As Samantha watched, the man threw a pebble into the water. She heard the sharp splash of it landing in the water. She immediately felt foolish for being disturbed by the sound. As she turned to walk away, the man shifted his gaze towards her. Only when she saw his face, slightly out of the shadows, did she realize who it was. Jacob, the maintenance worker who did odd jobs around Sage Gardens. She felt relieved that he wasn't just some vagrant that had somehow wandered into Sage Gardens.

"Hello, Samantha," Jacob said. He locked eyes with her. Samantha was surprised that he knew her name. She hadn't really spoken to him since he was only hired recently and she didn't often have a job that needed to be done in her villa that she couldn't do herself. As she studied him, his lips curved into a slow smile. "Not so wise to be out so late alone."

Samantha felt an icy wave wash over her. Something in his voice made her think that he was threatening her.

"Are you working?" Samantha asked. It wasn't until after she said it that she realized how rude she sounded. "I mean, do you often stay so late?"

"I'm just taking a little time before I head home. I need to rest a bit. It's a long drive. I'm sorry if I bothered you." He smiled again. This time his smile seemed genuine. "Do you want me to walk with you, wherever you are going?"

Samantha immediately warmed to him at the offer. It wasn't often that men of the younger generation still remembered the simple courtesies that their fathers and grandfathers had displayed.

"No, thank you. I can make it on my own." She returned his smile and began to walk away.

"It's not safe you know, to be out all alone," Jacob's voice carried along her spine. She glanced back over her shoulder almost expecting him to be pouncing on top of her. Instead he was casually reclining in his chair. He tossed another pebble into the water. Samantha stared at him a moment longer. She knew that she was being paranoid. Jacob had probably heard about the murder and was offering her good advice. She turned and hurried towards Eddy's villa. She wasn't sure if Jacob's words had spooked her, or if she was just starting to think he was right. When she reached Eddy's villa she knocked hard on the door.

A moment later the door jerked open.

"Samantha, what's wrong?" Eddy asked. His eyes filled with concern as he took in the sight of her. Samantha realized that she must have looked terrified. She pushed past him into the villa.

"Sorry, I got a little nervous."

"You? Nervous?" Eddy looked at her with wonder. "I didn't think that was possible."

"Please Eddy, I don't want to talk about it," Samantha mumbled. She made sure that the door was closed tightly behind her. Even though she had no real reason to be frightened, she still felt very on edge.

"Hey, whatever you want." Eddy studied her for a moment longer. "I know better than to argue with you."

"Ah, if only that were true." Samantha managed a laugh and shook her head. "So, what did you want to show me?"

Eddy hesitated as if he might want to press the topic of what she was afraid of during her walk. Then he turned to his kitchen table. "Do you remember those pictures we took of the footprints?"

"I remember. One by my side door, and one by Vince's body," Samantha said.

"I had a hard time seeing them clearly on my computer, so I decided to have them printed out." Eddy pointed to the photographs on the table. "I had it done at the police station so I could have the highest quality photographs I could get. A few things are clear to me now."

"What things?" Samantha asked.

"Look at these pictures." Eddy stared down at the photographs on the table.

"You had them blown up?" Samantha asked. She rested her hands on the table and leaned closer.

"I did. Because something about them was really bugging me. This first one is from the ground behind your villa, where the backpack was taken. This one is from the ground beside the bus driver's body. I didn't think too much of it at first, I knew that anyone could have walked in that area. Now, that I've looked at them more closely and measured them, I am certain that they match." He frowned. "I wish I could have used the program at the police station to analyze them, but my retired cop status doesn't always get me far enough. If my buddy had been working in the lab I could have gotten it, but he wasn't in."

"I don't think that you need a program to show that they are the same." Samantha pointed to the similar curve. "It's pretty clear." Samantha furrowed her brow. "Do you think that they are

Simon's?"

"Not unless he has a magic shrinking pill." Eddy smiled a little at his own dry humor. "Look how small those feet are. They can't be more than a size ten tops. I'm pretty sure that with Simon's gigantic feet he has to specially order his shoes."

"You're right." Samantha nodded as she recalled the time she had nearly tripped over Simon's feet. He had been tending the small garden on the side of the office building and just as she had rounded the corner he was stretching one leg out. They had managed to avoid a collision, but she had gotten a very good glimpse of the size of his foot. "He has to be beyond anything a regular store would sell. So, what do you think? Does this eliminate him as a suspect?"

"I think it makes him unlikely and I didn't like him for it in the first place, but no, I can't say it rules him out. What we have here are footprints in a heavily frequented area. If we were to look hard enough we would probably find yours in both places as well. But you're not the killer."

"Oh! Maybe a witness?" Samantha's eyes widened. "What if someone saw the crime, but is too afraid to come forward?"

"That's possible." Eddy picked up the photographs from the table. "But that doesn't explain why they were behind the bushes by your window. Although, maybe the backpack had nothing to do with the murder."

"Maybe." Samantha nodded.

"What I am fairly sure of is that if we find the owner of these shoes, we might be able to find more information about the owner of the backpack and about this murder."

"Shall we have a fitting for everyone that lives in Sage Gardens?" Samantha laughed shortly. "I don't think anyone is going to go for that unless we stage some kind of ball."

"Oh, the idea." Eddy shook his head. "You know how much the women around here like to dress up."

"I do." Samantha grinned. "I wonder if we

could get Walt to do the measuring."

"Could you imagine Walt with all of those stinky, sweaty feet?" Eddy laughed out loud. "I think he would end up passing out before he measured the first foot."

Samantha also laughed as she pictured Walt fainting in front of a big, sweaty foot. It was just what she needed to shake off the fear of her walk to Eddy's villa. She felt much better as her laughter died down.

"Okay, so we certainly can't measure everyone's foot in Sage Gardens. Besides, we don't know for sure if the killer is someone who lives in Sage Gardens. Just because the body was here, doesn't mean that it couldn't have been an outsider who committed the crime." She tapped her chin lightly. "No, I think we can assume that whoever's footprints these are is likely someone who did not live here. I've never seen any of the residents having trouble with Vince. In fact the only out of the ordinary thing I recall seeing was when he was flirting with Lily."

"Lily? The new office assistant?" Eddy questioned. "She seems nice enough. I've never noticed them flirting, but then I'm not sure I even know what flirting looks like."

Samantha guessed that he hadn't the faintest clue, but she kept that to herself.

"I asked Walt to come over and have a look, too. You know with his attention to detail he should be able to tell for sure if they match." Eddy walked over to the front door just as someone knocked. He opened it and Walt stepped inside.

"Samantha." He nodded to her with a hint of nervousness. Samantha offered him a warm smile to put him at ease.

"Here are the pictures." Eddy gestured to the photographs on the table.

"They look the same to me. What do you think, Walt?" Samantha looked over at him.

"They don't just look the same. They are the same." Walt pointed out a faint pattern in the mud. "That's from the sole of the shoe. I would say a shoe with a fairly worn down sole. The wear patterns match. There is no way two different shoes would have the exact same wear pattern."

"You can tell all of that from this?" Samantha asked. "That's amazing."

"Thank you," Walt replied smiling with genuine warmth. "Does anyone have any ideas about who these shoes might belong to?"

"They're small enough to possibly be a woman's," Samantha observed.

"Some men have small feet." Eddy glanced down at his own shoes.

"Really, there isn't enough of an outer rim to know the exact size of the shoe." Walt pointed to where the edge of the footprint faded into the soil. "It is possible that the shoe is a few inches longer, though certainly no more than that."

"So, it still rules out Simon." Samantha felt a sense of validation. "I knew he couldn't have been the one who did this.

"I wouldn't say that it rules him out entirely.

We don't even know if these footprints are connected to the murderer. What we have are assumptions that we are trying to connect together, but that does not equal evidence." Eddy tapped his finger lightly on one of the photographs. "But at least we have something."

"If the killer isn't Simon as the police suspect, do we have any idea who it might be?" Walt asked.

"Not really." Samantha shook her head slowly as she thought about it. "I've never noticed anyone arguing with Vince. To be honest I never noticed Vince much. But I would have if I saw him fighting with someone."

Samantha looked towards the window. She wondered if someone she knew was out there waiting to be arrested for murder.

"What about the office assistant, Lily?" Walt tapped his finger lightly on the table. "She's someone to look into."

"Lily? Why would you suspect her?" Samantha asked. She glanced away from the window towards Walt. "I've only seen Vince and

Lily being very friendly with one another."

"Yes, they used to be. But I've noticed Lily and Vince arguing a few times. It's not that I'm trying to be nosy, but when people are right there in the middle of the office and squabbling, it's hard not to notice." He frowned. "I actually noticed them arguing twice. I remember, exactly two times."

"Do you remember what they were arguing about?" Eddy asked.

"That, I don't know. I heard the anger in their voices, but I didn't hear exactly what they were saying. I can tell you that she seemed to be the angrier one. I think it at least warrants looking into. Even if she isn't the murderer she might have a more intimate knowledge of his associates." Walt frowned. "I do hate pointing fingers."

Samantha had grown very quiet. She seemed to be lost in thought. Eddy eyed her curiously. "What's going on in that head of yours?" he asked.

"I'm just thinking about something I saw about a month ago. I didn't think anything of it at the time. Now, that all of this has happened, and after what Walt said, I think maybe there was a lot to it." She frowned and shook her head. "I saw Lily and Vince in the parking lot beside the bus one morning. They weren't exactly being friendly, but they weren't arguing either. Vince gave Lily some money. It wasn't just like a twenty, it was a stack of cash. You don't see that too often anymore, that's why it stuck in my mind. I thought it was odd, but obviously it was none of my business, so I didn't ask any questions." She shook her head. "Maybe if I had paid more attention I could have figured out why they were exchanging money, but I didn't want them to notice that I noticed."

"There was no reason for you to be overly suspicious," Eddy commented. "But it's clear that Walt is right. Lily and Vince had a strong connection."

"But what kind of connection?" Samantha asked.

"Why would Vince be giving Lily money?" Eddy asked. "Maybe they were dating?"

"Even if they were, why would he be handing

her a stack of cash?" Walt questioned further. "I mean, sure couples exchange funds, but not in the middle of a parking lot. Unless things have changed vastly over the past twenty years, I don't recall stacks of cash being part of the courting ritual."

"Courting ritual?" Samantha raised an eyebrow. "Walt, things have definitely changed."

"I think we need to find out what Lily was up to with that money," Eddy spoke in a decisive tone. "Whatever it was, she should be able to tell us. If she doesn't, then we'll know she is trying to hide something."

"Well, she will have already gone home for the day more than likely," Samantha suggested.

"I'll go up and check. Maybe she stayed late. After all, if she and Vince were as close as we think, then she must have been impacted by the murder." Eddy nodded to Walt and Samantha as the three walked out of Eddy's villa. "Just be careful. The closer we get to figuring this out the more danger we could all be in."

As Eddy turned towards the office, Walt began to walk towards his villa. Samantha cleared her throat. Walt looked back at her.

"Are you okay, Samantha?" he asked.

"Do you think you could walk with me to my villa?" She frowned. She knew that it was the opposite direction, but she was still feeling spooked.

"Of course." Walt fell into step beside her. As they walked Samantha thought about the fights that Walt had witnessed.

"How do you know that Lily was the angrier of the two, Walt?"

"Well, she kept pointing her finger at him. She snapped her words. He was more cajoling, as if he was trying to convince her of something." He shrugged. "It's possible that I interpreted it wrong."

"No, I don't think that you did." Samantha frowned. "In fact it sounds like whatever was between them might have been intense."

"I imagine it was." Walt laughed a little. "Ah, to be young again and so concerned about every little thing, hmm?" He glanced over at her.

"I suppose." Samantha smiled a little. She had spent most of her younger years hunting stories and dodging the well-intentioned questions of her mother. She didn't regret the adventures she had. But once in a while she wondered about what might have been if she had chosen a different path.

"Here we are." Samantha looked over at Walt. "Thank you for walking me. I just feel a little nervous. Whoever took the backpack knew that it was left by my villa."

"Make sure you keep things locked up tight. Or if you want, you could stay with me tonight." Walt met her eyes. "I mean, if you're scared to be alone."

Samantha felt very touched. With how Walt needed everything to be a certain way and in a special order, she knew that it was a stretch for him to invite someone to be a house guest.

"Thank you, Walt. But I think I will be okay. Besides, you and Eddy are only a few villas away."

"That's right. If you need us, call us." Walt waved to her. "I'll see you tomorrow."

"Good night, Walt."

Samantha still had a smile on her face when she stepped into the villa. It was wonderful to have such good friends nearby.

Chapter Six

As Eddy walked up to the main office he noticed Owen walking towards the parking lot. Owen was the nurse that the property manager had hired to tend to residents on a daily basis. It was easier than driving to the doctor for simple check-ups or minor injuries. It was one of the perks that Sage Gardens offered, especially for the older residents.

"Owen!" Eddy wanted to catch him before he reached the parking lot. Owen turned towards the sound of Eddy's voice.

"How are you doing, Eddy?" Owen asked. "I haven't seen you around much lately."

"I got caught up in this new television show." Eddy smiled a little.

"I doubt that." Owen eyed Eddy curiously. "Have you been feeling all right?"

"Just a little more tired than usual." Eddy sighed with the admission. He hated to show any

85

sign of weakness. In his mind he was still thirty years old and fit enough to pass the police fitness test.

"Could be your sugar, or your blood pressure, let me check you out." Owen gestured to the small office where he saw residents.

"No really I'm fine, you were just leaving." Eddy shook his head.

"Nonsense, if you've been avoiding me, there's a reason." Owen opened the door to the office. Eddy smiled some. Owen had become a bit of a surrogate son to Eddy and he appreciated that Owen had taken such an interest. "In with you!" Owen pointed to the office and then stepped inside. Eddy chuckled and followed him inside.

"Thanks, Owen." Eddy sat down on the small padded exam table.

"So, how long have you been experiencing exhaustion?" Owen asked. He wrapped a blood pressure cuff around Eddy's arm.

"Ever since I met Samantha," Eddy replied in

a dry tone.

Owen met his eyes with a short laugh. "Are you pulling my leg, Eddy?"

"Honestly, I haven't been tired. I've been laying low because some new single ladies have moved in. You know how they like the men in uniform." He winked lightly at Owen.

"So, that must mean that you wanted to get me alone for another reason?" Owen asked.

"Aha, you are starting to pick up on the detective skills," Eddy lowered his voice slightly. "I wanted to talk about Vince."

"Vince." Owen nodded. "It's a terrible thing, what happened to him. I still can't wrap my head around Simon being involved."

"Neither can I. I don't think he was." Eddy frowned and leaned closer. "What I'm trying to figure out is, who was? Samantha said she saw Vince talking to Lily a few times. Walt mentioned that he had seen them argue. Did you notice anything strange between them?"

"Between them, no." Owen put the blood pressure cuff away. He looked a little tense as he turned back to Eddy.

"Between whom then?" Eddy pressed.

"To be honest with you, I'd rather not say." Owen set his jaw.

"Owen, this is me." Eddy looked at him with disbelief. "You can tell me what you suspect."

"It's not that I don't trust you, Eddy, it's just I've tried to make it my policy to not spread rumors." Owen sighed. "I mean, if you share a rumor enough times it pretty much becomes the truth. This rumor could get someone in a lot of trouble."

Eddy was intrigued. He stood up from the padded bench.

"Well, I think Vince got into plenty of trouble. Don't you?" He met Owen's eyes directly, leaving him no room to argue. "If what you know might have anything to do with that, I suggest you tell me."

Owen shook his head as he looked at Eddy. "I bet you were fierce in the interrogation room."

"That's putting it mildly," Eddy's tone was hard as he continued to fix Owen with a steady gaze. "So?"

Owen peeked his head out the door of the office to make sure that no one was nearby. Then he closed the door again. He turned back to look at Eddy.

"You have to understand that when you work with people, there's a certain sense of loyalty." Owen frowned.

"That loyalty goes out the window when someone ends up dead." Eddy clenched his jaw briefly, and then released a sigh. "Listen, it's me, Owen. I'll keep your name out of anything this might turn into. Okay?"

"Okay." Owen nodded, but he still appeared reluctant. "Petty cash has been going missing over the past month or so. There are rumors that Lily is stealing it. So far no one has been able to prove it. But she is the main suspect."

"Lily?" Eddy asked. "That's surprising."

"Isn't it?" Owen's eyes widened. "I didn't want to believe it at first. She's always so sweet and seems to really care about the residents here. But I've got to admit that the more rumors I hear the more I begin to wonder. I mean, who else could it be?"

"Hmm." Eddy narrowed his eyes. "That is a good question. What about Vince? Did anyone suspect him of stealing?"

"I don't think there's any way he could have. The petty cash is locked in the safe and only a few staff members have the combination." Owen crossed his arms. "I don't know for sure that Lily was involved in stealing, but she did seem pretty cozy with Vince. Then again, she's friendly with everyone."

"Thanks for the information, Owen." Eddy opened the door.

"Just remember that I don't know anything for sure," Owen said firmly. Eddy smiled at him. He could always count on Owen's honesty, that was one of the first things that had bonded the two of them together. Now he was curious about Lily's behavior. Was it possible that Vince had found out about the stolen money and decided to turn her in? Would Lily be capable of killing someone to protect her job and her freedom?

Eddy frowned as he walked back towards his villa. It was never a good thing when a suspect list kept growing instead of getting smaller. It was going to take a lot of sorting to figure out exactly who was responsible. Unfortunately for Simon, he was the easiest target. Eddy had worked with many detectives who believed the simplest answer was usually always the right answer. He knew that Detective Brunner would probably be inclined to go after Simon if there was adequate evidence rather than looking for any other suspects.

Chapter Seven

Early the next morning Samantha received a call from Eddy.

"I want to speak with Lily. Do you want to join me?" Eddy asked.

"Yes, I have a few questions for her, too. I'll meet you there." She hung up the phone before Eddy could argue. She was used to him thinking that he could always take the lead in things like this, and she was going to make sure that he knew that he couldn't. When she met up with him outside the office he regarded her warily.

"Morning, Samantha."

"Morning, Eddy." She smiled at him. "Did you find out any information last night?"

"Only that Lily may be a thief." Eddy tilted his head towards the door of the office. "I'm going to go in there and find out one way or the other." He held Samantha's eyes as if awaiting a challenge from her.

"I think that you should let me do the talking." Samantha shot a look in his direction.

"You? Why? I'm the one with experience." Eddy shook his head. "I did this for a living remember?"

"You were trained to get information out of someone you had trapped in a box. You used intimidation and force to get your answers. In my career I had to get information from people by being as kind and often as manipulative as possible. People don't willingly speak to a crime reporter you know, I had to be quite charismatic," she said confidently as they neared the office.

"That I believe." Eddy winked lightly at her. "You have enough charm to get anyone to do anything."

Samantha regarded him for a moment. She wasn't sure whether to take his words as a compliment or as an insult. Either way she was fairly certain that she was not going to find a way to convince him to let her take the lead.

"Listen Eddy, women don't like to be cornered

and questioned. We don't have any real evidence against Lily. The moment she thinks that you're accusing her of something, she's going to turn tail and run," Samantha emphasized. "If we go in there with guns blazing we're both just going to be wasting our time."

"Just let me do what I do, Samantha. You have to learn to trust me sometime," he smiled faintly at her.

Samantha raised an eyebrow and was about to explain that she did trust him but some things should be left to her, but it was too late. Eddy was already opening the door to the office. Lily hung up her cell phone the moment they walked in. She was a young and petite woman. Her wavy, light brown hair was always perfect and her nails were pristine. She took care of herself very well. Samantha had asked her a few times about the shade of lipstick she wore or where she had her nails done, as Lily always looked so beautiful. Samantha didn't preoccupy herself with things like that, but once in a while she liked to make the extra effort to look nice.

"Hi Lily," Eddy spoke up before Samantha could. "Do you have a minute to talk?"

"Uh, Eddy, right?" Lily asked. "You're a friend of Owen's, aren't you?"

"Yes." Eddy nodded and offered her what he hoped was a charming smile. "I just need to ask you a few questions."

That sentence caused her lips to tighten and her eyes to harden. She looked from Eddy to Samantha and then back to Eddy. "About what?"

"Oh, just a few things we want to clear up," Samantha said in a softer tone. She wanted to put Lily at ease since it was clear that Eddy had already ruffled her feathers. "Do you think we could sit?" She gestured to the two chairs in front of the desk.

"Oh, I wish I had the time, but I was actually just heading out. I hope you understand. If you have any complaints about the property I can give you the manager's number." She smiled. When

Lily smiled her entire face lit up and she looked even younger. She had cherubic features that gave her an air of innocence.

"I'm sure you can answer these questions quickly. Don't you have a minute or two?" Eddy asked. His voice was stern enough that his words didn't sound very much like questions. Lily looked at him with mounting suspicion.

"I don't know what this is about, but I have to go." Lily stood up from behind the desk. "Like I said, I'd be happy to give you the manager's number if you need to speak to someone right away. Is there a maintenance problem? I can call Jacob for you."

Samantha cringed at the mention of Jacob. She recalled the way he had looked at her when she walked past him. The last thing she wanted was Jacob's help.

"No, we don't need Jacob. We need to speak to you." Samantha decided to say something before Eddy could get more aggressive and frighten Lily. "Weren't you friends with Vince?"

Lily lowered her eyes a moment. She nodded silently.

"We are only here to help, Lily," Samantha spoke in a softer tone. She stepped closer to Lily. "I can only imagine what a shock it was for you to hear the news."

Lily looked up at Samantha with tears in her eyes. "I really can't talk now," her voice trembled with each word.

"I understand. We're not trying to cause you any trouble, Lily. We just wanted to know if you knew anything about what Vince might have been involved in. Was he in with a dangerous crowd?" Samantha met Lily's eyes with genuine sympathy. But whatever bond Lily had begun to form with Samantha immediately snapped.

"I said I don't have time to talk. All you want to do is spread rumors. Vince was a good man, and no one should be talking behind his back." Lily whisked by Samantha. "I have to go."

"Lily wait!" Samantha started to go after her, but Eddy grabbed her lightly by the wrist.

"Don't bother. We're not going to get anything else out of her right now." He frowned.

"What are we going to do?" Samantha sighed. "We didn't find anything out."

"Samantha, would you say that Lily might just be hiding something?" Eddy's voice held a hint of sarcasm.

"I'd have to say, yes. The question is, what?" Samantha asked. "She was in an awfully big hurry to get out of here."

"Well, then maybe we should follow her." Eddy pulled his keys out of his pocket. "Care to join me for a drive?"

"Absolutely." Samantha smiled. She was chomping at the bit to find out what Lily was up to.

"Let's hurry," Eddy said leading her towards the parking lot. Lily's car was just pulling out when Eddy and Samantha got into Eddy's car. Eddy did his best to appear casual and waited a minute before pulling out as well. The road leading out of Sage Gardens was long and had no other turns until it reached the main road. Eddy could afford to leave Lily a little space.

"Where do you think she's going?" Samantha asked.

"Maybe to a doctor's appointment. Maybe to meet with a lawyer. Who knows?" Eddy peered through the windshield and kept a close eye on the tail lights of Lily's car.

"Did you do this often?" Samantha asked.

"Do what?" Eddy glanced briefly at her.

"Tail criminals?" Samantha grinned. "You seem very good at it."

"Not really." Eddy chuckled. "My career as a police officer wasn't as exciting as the shows you see on television. Before I became a detective it mostly involved driving around in circles and waiting for a call to come through and then I spent a lot of time investigating and interrogating. But there were times that I was involved in some situations that were quite tense." His expression grew solemn. "There are moments I wish I hadn't lived, trust me."

Samantha grew quiet as she studied his profile. Eddy was often brusque but occasionally he gave her a glimpse of what his inner world was like. She could tell that there were things that haunted him. She hoped that one day he would consider her a good enough friend to confide some of those things. As far as Samantha knew, she, Walt, and Owen, were Eddy's only real friends. He had many contacts in the police department, but none of them seemed to be his friends.

"I'm sure you had some experiences that you wish you could undo," Eddy commented turning the car to follow after Lily.

"I did," Samantha agreed. "I have to say everything felt tense, you know? Sometimes situations seemed a lot more dramatic than they actually were. But I was always waiting for things to get hairy."

"You are one brave woman, Samantha." Eddy

looked over at her with a brief smile. "Or foolish, I'm not sure just yet."

"Oh, thanks for that almost compliment." Samantha laughed. "Oh look, she's turning into that plaza." Samantha pointed through the side window.

"Great, we tailed her to her manicurist." Eddy shook his head as one of the shops in the plaza was a hair and nail salon. He started to drive past the plaza as he didn't see a reason to continue following her. Samantha grabbed the crook of his elbow.

"Turn in!" Her words were hissed with urgency. Eddy was startled by her tone and almost took the curb when he turned into the entrance of the plaza. He managed to straighten the car without losing control of it, but his cheeks were red with anger.

"Samantha, you could have gotten us both killed," Eddy said sharply as he looked over at her. He pulled the car into the parking lot.

"She didn't go into the salon." Samantha

frowned. "She went around behind the building."

"So, maybe there is more parking back there?" Eddy suggested.

"Why would she need more parking? The place is practically empty." Samantha pointed to all of the empty parking spots right in front of the salon. Eddy nodded a little.

"That's still no reason to nearly kill us." Eddy steered the car slowly around the side of the building.

"I'm sorry, I just reacted." Samantha's gaze was fixated to the window. "I am certain she is up to something. Every secret meeting I've ever heard of takes place in an empty parking lot."

"I can't disagree with you there." Eddy nodded. He stopped the car at the corner of the building. "If we pull all the way around she's going to know that we're here."

"On foot?" Samantha asked.

"Only if you promise to listen to me." Eddy met her eyes. "We have no idea what Lily is up to.

At the very least it's probably something to do with the money. She may be stealing from petty cash. At worst it could have something to do with Vince's murder. If you're not going to listen to me, then you need to stay in the car."

"Oh Eddy!" Samantha looked at him with a soft smile. "You're so sweet and naive."

Eddy stared at her with confusion. "What?"

"To think that anyone gets to tell me what to do." Samantha smirked. She climbed out of the car before Eddy could stop her. She had been in enough dangerous situations to handle herself, and she had never been armed in any of them. As she crept towards the corner of the building, Eddy caught up with her. He shot her a glare, but didn't argue. He peered around the corner as well. There were only two cars behind the building, Lily's and a brown sedan.

As Samantha and Eddy watched, the driver's side door of the brown sedan swung open. A man stepped out, dressed in one of the most ridiculous suits that Samantha had ever seen. That was saying a lot considering the places that she had been. The suit was mostly white with splashes of color on the lapels, stripes on the pants, and a neon yellow dress shirt under the jacket. She had never seen anything like it before. The hat perched on top of his head had a thin, short brim and was just as colorful as his suit.

As he walked towards Lily, Samantha felt some anxiety. What if Lily was in danger? What if they just stood there and watched as she got herself into a bad situation? Samantha looked over at Eddy. He was completely focused on the scene that was unfolding. Samantha knew how important it was to find out what Lily was up to, but she felt such an urge to intervene. Lily greeted the man with a slight nod. There wasn't a hint of affection, or even fear.

"Do you have it?" he asked sternly.

"I said I would, didn't I?" she spat her words in return. It was clear that there was no love lost between the two of them. Samantha could sense the tension building as they glared at one another.

Eddy handed his phone to Samantha and indicated to her to take a photo of the man.

"So? Where is it? I don't want you playing any more games with me, Lily," his voice carried across the parking lot. His words were rumbled in a way that made everything he said sound like a threat. Samantha positioned the phone and took a photo as she listened closely.

"I'm not playing any games," Lily said as she reached into her purse and pulled out a thick envelope. Samantha suspected that it had money stacked inside. As she watched, Lily handed it over to the man. "This is the final payment."

"All of it?" The man looked genuinely surprised. He flipped the envelope open and just as Samantha had suspected he lifted a stack of cash halfway out of the envelope. He began sorting through the bills. "Did you win the lottery?" He chuckled.

"That's not really any of your concern," Lily said sternly. "Our business is finished. I don't expect to hear from you again."

"That hurts, Lily," he said mockingly. "After all I've done for you, that's how you treat me?"

"Goodbye." She turned and started to walk back towards her car. Samantha's heart fell. She had hoped that Lily would turn out to be innocent, but from the way it looked, she was definitely involved.

"We should go," Eddy hissed beside Samantha's ear. "We don't want them knowing that we were here."

Samantha nodded. She looked once more in Lily's direction. Then she followed Eddy to the car. As Eddy sped out of the parking lot, Samantha stared out the window.

"What's wrong?" Eddy asked. He looked over at her with some concern. "I'm not used to you being so quiet."

"It just seems to me that Lily hired that man to kill Vince. I mean it's the only thing that makes sense, isn't it? The way she said that their business was finished. It made me sick to my stomach to think that she could have hired someone to slaughter Vince." She closed her eyes briefly. "I really wanted her to be as nice as she seemed."

"Wait a minute, pump the brakes." Eddy shook his head. "You're making an awful lot of assumptions."

"Am I? What else could it be about?" Samantha replied. "She was stealing from petty cash to pay for Vince's murder. It's disgusting. In a way our rent probably funded a murder for hire."

"If that's what happened." Eddy pulled back into Sage Gardens. "Things are not always as they seem, Samantha. I didn't peg Lily for a killer."

"I didn't peg her for one either, but that doesn't mean that she isn't." Samantha sighed. "It's much easier to pay someone to do your dirty work than to do it yourself."

"But it's also possible that Lily was paying him for something else, like drugs." Eddy frowned. "We still don't know what happened to that cocaine, or even where it came from. She might have bought it from the man in the parking lot, and needed to pay her debt for it."

"That's true." Samantha nodded slowly.

"The best way to find out what she was doing with him, is to find out who he is. We've got his picture, I'm going to take it to one of my guys in the lab at the police station. He can run it through facial recognition and we might get a hit. I find it very unlikely that he doesn't have a criminal history." He parked the car.

"That's a good idea." Samantha opened her car door to get out.

"Samantha, wait just a minute," Eddy asked. He looked at her with a pleading expression.

"What is it?" She turned back to look at him.

"Listen, I know that sometimes I get a little forceful. Old habits die hard. No hard feelings?" He met her eyes with concern. Samantha was touched that he seemed worried about whether he had offended her.

"No hard feelings. Just remember, next time I'm putting you on your back." She smiled saucily and closed the car door behind her. As she walked away she could hear him chuckling behind her. Her friendship with Eddy had its strained moments, but she was beginning to see that he really only had the best intentions.

Chapter Eight

Eddy was still troubled by the way he had spoken to Samantha as he drove to the local police station. He knew that a young lab tech, Chris, would be working, and he wanted to be there in person to make sure that he would evaluate the photograph that Samantha had taken. He parked in the public lot and walked up to the police station. He noticed a few looks from officers and staff that recognized him, but he didn't stop to talk. Instead he just kept walking towards the lab. He knew that at any moment someone might stop him as he was entering a private area, but he didn't care. If he was questioned then he would explain himself, otherwise he would just keep going. As he reached the lab Chris was just stepping inside. He paused when he saw Eddy.

"Eddy!" He smiled from ear to ear. "It's so good to see you."

"And you." Eddy smiled in return. "I'm sorry I haven't dropped in much lately."

"Hey, that's all right. What can I help you with?" Chris lifted an eyebrow. "I know that you're not here just for a visit."

"Actually, I have a picture of someone. I was hoping that you could run it through the facial recognition program, if it's not too much trouble."

"No trouble at all." Chris glanced around as if he was looking for someone in particular, then he gestured to the door of the lab. "Go ahead. We'll upload the picture and get the program started."

"Great." Eddy stepped into the lab. He noticed that Chris looked around again before shutting the door. The door did not provide much privacy as the lab was mostly windows.

Not long after Eddy uploaded the photograph to Chris' computer there was a swift, sharp knock on the door of the lab. Chris looked up fearfully. Eddy followed his gaze to the face in the window of the door.

"Oops, looks like I've been spotted," Eddy muttered as Detective Brunner opened the door to the lab.

"What's going on in here?" Detective Brunner asked. His annoyance was clearly depicted by the crease in his forehead and the curl of his upper lip.

"Nothing of interest." Eddy met the detective's eyes without hesitation.

"You don't have clearance to be in the lab." Detective Brunner gestured to the door. "Leave please!"

Eddy gritted his teeth, but he did not argue. He didn't want to do anything that would put Chris' job in jeopardy. Once he was out in the hallway, Detective Brunner followed after him.

"Look, Chris is a friend, I was just visiting." Eddy frowned.

"I don't believe that at all." Detective Brunner narrowed his eyes. "I think you're poking your nose into things."

"Shouldn't I?" Eddy raised an eyebrow. "I don't see you doing the job properly."

"Excuse me?" Detective Brunner shook his head. "We have a suspect in custody."

"Wrong, you have an innocent man in custody." Eddy tried to stay calm as he didn't want to antagonize Detective Brunner unnecessarily. "When the truth comes out you're going to have a scandal on your hands." Eddy eyed him grimly.

"And you know this, how?" Detective Brunner asked.

"I think you need to do a more thorough investigation." He fixed Detective Brunner with a hard gaze. "I don't think this murder is as simple as it seems. You need to stop rushing it and look into it further."

"Or maybe you need to remember that you are retired." He pointed to the exit. "Now leave, before you get arrested."

Eddy stared at him with disbelief. He felt an extreme urge to get into a scuffle with the man, but he forced himself to resist. He would never sully the sanctity of a police station with violent behavior.

"I'll leave, just remember what I said." Eddy sneered with disgust. As he walked out of the police station he felt a pang of regret. He missed belonging to the police force, he missed the detectives he had once known and worked with, who would have turned every rock to make sure the murder was adequately investigated and solved. He felt as if so much had changed since he wore the badge. Despite the fact that he was no longer a detective, the obligation he felt to seek justice still weighed on him just as heavily as it always had.

Samantha was waiting for Eddy in front of his villa when he returned.

"Where have you been?" She noticed the troubled look on his face.

"I took the photograph into the police lab to have it analyzed for facial recognition." He unlocked his door and opened it for her.

"What happened?" Samantha followed him in. "Did you get a match?"

"No match yet. I don't think." He frowned and tossed his keys into a small ceramic bowl on the table and placed his hat on the coat rack. "I should hear soon."

"Are you doing okay, Eddy?" Samantha asked. He had barely looked at her.

"Yes, I just wish that we were a little closer to finding the actual killer. I mean we have theories, but none of them really hold water yet. We need the missing pieces."

"I know you're frustrated. So am I," Samantha said. "I hate to admit it, but I'm not comfortable in my own home. I keep thinking about what will happen if the killer is spooked."

"Samantha, you shouldn't have to worry about that. I will do my best to make sure that you don't have to." Eddy looked as if he was about to say more, but the ring of his cell phone interrupted him.

Eddy picked up his cell phone on the first ring.

"What do you have for me?"

"I have the identity of the man in the picture you gave me," Chris said. "He's a well-known loan shark."

"A loan shark?" Eddy asked.

"Doesn't that sound right to you?" Chris sounded troubled. He was always eager to please Eddy.

"No, I'm sure it's right, it's just not what I expected. Did he have any involvement with drugs in the past?"

"No, nothing like that."

"What about working as a hitman? Or even hired muscle?" Eddy suggested.

"No, his only arrests have been non-violent," Chris insisted. "I don't even see any known associates that were involved in violent crime or drugs. He seems to be purely a financial predator."

"Thanks for your help, Chris."

"I'm sorry if I didn't get you the answers that you're looking for."

"You did great, Chris. Thanks a lot."

"What did he say?" Samantha asked eagerly as Eddy hung up his phone. He looked puzzled as he thought about what Chris had told him.

"It seems that our drug dealing hitman is neither. He's just a loan shark." He shrugged.

"A loan shark?" Samantha pursed her lips for a moment as she replayed in her mind the encounter they had witnessed. "So, the money she gave him was likely to pay off a loan."

"Well, we don't know that for sure. It's possible that he branched off into more violent activity recently. It's unlikely given his lack of violent history, but it's always possible."

"I suppose. It just seems like we're going around in circles with this." She sighed.

"There's really only one way to find out exactly what he was up to. We can go to him and ask him." Eddy smiled.

"As if it's that simple?" Samantha laughed at the idea. "I don't think that he's going to talk that easily."

"Maybe not, but we won't know unless we ask, will we? I can have Chris text me some of the places he frequents. I don't think that it will take us long to find him, as outlandish as his style is." He chuckled at the memory of it.

"That's true. I suppose that it couldn't hurt to try. Shall we go together?"

"I was hoping you'd agree." He picked his keys up out the bowl. "I'll drive."

"All right." Samantha nodded. As they walked towards the parking lot, Walt waved to them from the office. The three met in the middle of the courtyard.

"Where are you two off to?" Walt asked.

"We're going to pay a visit to a loan shark." Eddy looked towards the office. "Were you in the office?"

"Yes, I was just giving Lily my rent check," he said as he ushered the two of them away from the office. "I just saw Lily on one of those online poker sites," he whispered.

"Really?" Eddy asked with wide eyes.

"Yep." Walt nodded. "When she saw I was there she quickly closed down the page."

"Maybe she is involved in gambling," Samantha said thoughtfully.

"Maybe that's why she needed the money," Eddy suggested.

"Yeah, maybe she has a gambling problem," Walt agreed.

"So, Lily was gambling?" Samantha said thoughtfully. "Maybe she got in too deep and that's why she borrowed money from the loan shark."

"That still doesn't explain why she killed Vince, or if she did. I think we still need to talk to the loan shark." Eddy glanced at Walt. "Want to come along?"

"No, thank you. I don't do seedy well." He shook his head sharply.

Samantha tried not to laugh at his reaction.

"Okay, we'll let you know what we find out,"

Eddy promised.

***

Eddy and Samantha stopped at several clubs and hangouts throughout the city. It was getting to be very late by the time they stopped at the last potential location for the loan shark. The parking lot was half-filled with cars. It was just getting to be happy hour, and Samantha was sure that more people would be arriving soon.

"Might be crowded." Eddy frowned as he stepped out of the car.

"I don't think that he'll be very hard to spot." Samantha smiled at Eddy and climbed out the passenger side.

"Let's hope that you're right," Eddy replied. He slid his arm through Samantha's as they walked up to the building. On the outside it just looked like an abandoned strip mall. But when Eddy opened the door flashing lights and throbbing music poured out of the luxurious interior. Everything was carpeted. The floors, the seats, and the walls. To Samantha, it felt like being swallowed up by carpet. The music was loud and pounding.

Samantha had been in places like this in the past, but had no good memories of them. It was easy to get into trouble when the lights were too dim to see who was lurking, and the music was too loud for anyone to hear a scream. She was relieved to feel Eddy's arm hooked snugly in her own. As if he was thinking the same thing he tightened his grasp. Samantha did not resist. She searched the crowd for any sign of the man they were looking for.

"There he is." Samantha tilted her head towards the multi-colored hat that stuck out in a group of dark hats and bare heads. They walked a bit closer as Eddy removed his arm from hers so they could fit through the crowd. "Looks like he has quite a few friends," Samantha said as he was surrounded by several other men. They were laughing and joking loudly.

Samantha felt her muscles tense. Confronting a loan shark was one thing, but doing so while he was surrounded by potentially unsavoury people was quite another. "Should we wait it out?" she said as she turned towards Eddy only to find that he was no longer beside her. When she looked back at the loan shark she realized that Eddy had already inserted himself in the group of men, and was laughing right along with them. Samantha might have been annoyed if she wasn't so impressed.

Samantha made her way casually towards the group, but remained on the edge of the gathering. She knew that it would be quite strange for a lone woman to walk up to that many men when she knew none of them. She was close enough to hear their conversation, but far enough away to be just another patron of the club.

"So, what brings you here?" The loan shark slung an arm around Eddy's neck. "I don't think we've had an old legend in these parts in a long time."

Samantha raised an eyebrow. She had no idea what he meant by that.

"You know, I've been busy, Maury." Eddy shrugged.

"Well, it's good to see you, old man. I've heard so many stories about you. I'm just glad that I've never been across the table from you." He chuckled at that.

"Oh, but you are right now, Maury." Eddy locked eyes with the man. "There may not be a table, but we need to talk."

Maury's smile faded. He slowly drew his arm away from Eddy's shoulders. "What's this about?" he asked in a gruff tone.

"I want to know why you were meeting with Lily Cabressi." Eddy straightened his shoulders and stood his ground.

Maury looked over at his gaggle of friends. "Give us a minute."

His friends all began to scatter throughout the

club. Samantha took the opportunity to move closer to Eddy.

"Just some friendly questions, Maury." Eddy smiled.

"With you, Eddy, nothing is friendly." Maury shook his head. "I knew that woman would get me in trouble eventually."

"Hey, I don't want to cause any trouble. I'm just looking for some information." Eddy met his eyes again. "Nothing but a conversation."

"I don't believe you," Maury scowled. "But what is it that you want to know?"

"Lily, what was your business with her?" Eddy braced himself for Maury's response.

"My business, is my business, Eddy, and it has nothing to do with you. I thought you hung up the badge?" He glared at Eddy.

"We're not here as police." Samantha stepped up to the two men. "We're here because we're trying to free an innocent man."

Maury stared at Samantha for some time.

Eddy grimaced with barely restrained frustration at the interruption.

"A free man, eh?" Maury looked more intently at Samantha. "I'm all about freedom. Too many people getting locked up for no reason."

"Exactly." Samantha nodded. "All we need to know is why you were meeting with Lily."

Maury looked past the two as if searching for any backup they might have called in. Then he looked over at Eddy. "She owed me money, that's all."

"From a gambling debt?" Samantha suggested.

"Gambling is illegal outside of a casino, ma'am." Maury wagged his finger at her. "I don't ask what the loans are for, I just try to help out my friends anytime I can. But you know, they have to pay me back eventually."

"Or your friends start losing appendages?" Eddy muttered.

"My business is my business, Eddy. It's all

between friends." He crossed his arms.

"All right, fine. So, you loaned her a large sum of money?" Eddy asked.

"It was quite a bit, yes." He nodded.

"Did she ever mention a man named Vince?" Samantha asked.

"No, we didn't really discuss anything beyond the cash. She was having a hard time paying it back. But we're all settled up now, no worries."

"Even if the money she paid you with came from committing a murder?" Samantha challenged.

"Samantha," Eddy spoke sternly.

"Look hon, I don't care where the money comes from as long as it ends up in my pocket. All right? Now, if you two are going to start slinging around the big M word, this conversation is over. I'm not getting any murder pinned on me." Maury turned and walked away. Samantha started to go after him.

"Don't you even think about it," Eddy warned.

"He won't tell you anything else. When he decides a conversation is over, it is over."

"But I'm sure that there is more that he could tell us," Samantha stated firmly as she watched Maury disappear into the crowd.

"I'm sure you're right. He might have told us a lot more, if you hadn't interrupted us." He turned towards the door and glanced back. He expected her to follow. Samantha felt terrible as she trailed after him. She thought she was helping, but she was also trying to take over. She wanted the chance to question Maury as much as Eddy did.

Outside, Eddy opened the passenger door for Samantha. "Let's get out of here before Maury comes back with his friends."

Samantha slid into the seat silently. She didn't even bother to look in his direction. After Eddy started the car and got on the road, Samantha's mind shifted back to the encounter between Eddy and Maury.

"You didn't tell me that you knew Maury."

"Did I need to?" Eddy's response was short.

"No, I was just surprised that you two seemed to know each other quite well." She sighed. "Are you going to stay angry with me?"

"I'm not angry. I just wish that you would trust me to do my job. Yes, Maury and I knew each other in the past. I didn't recognize him until I saw him properly face to face. I didn't think he would remember me. We worked on a small potatoes sting together years ago. He got paid for it, and we went our separate ways. It was nothing really. When he recognized me, I just went with it." He shook his head. "You may know how to get information out of people, Samantha, but when it comes to a loan shark like Maury you have to be very careful about what words you use. The moment that you mentioned murder, he wasn't going to say another word."

"I'm sorry," Samantha apologized and looked out the window. "I guess I got a little ahead of myself."

"Don't feel too badly. I don't think he had

much more to tell us. He loaned Lily a large amount of money, probably to pay off her gambling debt to someone else. I'm just not sure how Vince is involved in any of this."

"Remember, Vince gave Lily money. Maybe he had a loan from Maury, too." She clucked her tongue lightly. "I don't know if we're going to figure out how this all connects."

"We will," Eddy spoke with confidence. "There's one person who knows the truth about everything. It's time we speak to her again. I want you to meet me at the office first thing tomorrow morning. We're not going to let Lily slip away this time."

Chapter Nine

Samantha had trouble sleeping. Her mind kept returning to the look in Lily's eyes. Her thoughts were a muddle of suspicion. She had no idea who to suspect anymore. The thought of Simon still being in jail weighed on her mind as well. She tossed and turned most of the night.

When the sun began to rise she remembered that she needed to get up and meet Eddy. She decided to close her eyes for just a moment. That moment passed very quickly. When she opened her eyes again it had been almost an hour. She jumped out of bed. Half-asleep she rummaged through her closet for something to put on. Then she rushed out the door. Her fingers stumbled over the menus on her phone in an attempt to see if she had missed a call from Eddy. When she reached the office, she didn't see him waiting for her outside. She hurried towards the door. At the same time she typed out a text to Eddy.

Where are you?

She looked up in time to see two figures through the front office window. It only took her a second to recognize one as Lily and the other as Eddy. Her stomach lurched as she realized that Eddy was already inside. Samantha jerked the door open and stepped inside.

"Samantha, do you want to call off your dog?" Lily asked. Her eyes were shining with fury as she glared at Eddy.

"Dog?" Eddy shot back. "I don't think that you have a right to be insulting me when Vince is laying dead in a morgue somewhere. Do you think you had nothing to do with that?"

Samantha cringed as the tension between the two increased. "Lily, we all just want to figure out what happened to Vince. That's all," Samantha kept her voice soft in an attempt to soothe the nerves of both of them.

"Really? Like either of you care about Vince?"

Lily snapped. "I've never even seen either of you speak to him. But all of a sudden you're best friends?"

"We know that you're stealing," Eddy growled. "It doesn't take much to go from a thief to a murderer, now does it?"

"What?" Lily shrieked. "You keep quiet! You have no idea what you're talking about! I would never hurt Vince!" Lily's eyes brimmed with tears. Her hands balled into fists at her sides as if she might decide to haul off and punch Eddy right in the nose. Instead, her tears began to fall. Her body trembled with the force of her grief. Samantha recognized her genuine sorrow.

"Oh Lily," she said gently. "You two were in love, weren't you?"

"You're falling for this?" Eddy asked incredulously.

Samantha shot him a look of impatience. Then she looked back at Lily. "I'm sorry that he's gone, Lily," she spoke gently.

Lily began to cry. Samantha grabbed a tissue from the desk and offered it to her. Lily took it and dabbed lightly at her eyes.

"I still can't believe it," she whispered. "I can't believe that he's gone, after all that we've been through."

Eddy shifted uncomfortably from one foot to the other. It was clear that he was still trying to adjust to the change of mood in the room.

"Just tell me what happened, Lily. I want to get justice for Vince, just like you do," Samantha said as soothingly as she could.

"Vince and I were together a while ago. We were going to get married. But things didn't work out. Even though we weren't engaged anymore, we still remained best friends. When I started having problems, I turned to Vince to help me." She wiped at her eyes and shook her head. "I didn't ever think that it would come to this. I don't know what happened to Vince, I only hope it wasn't my fault."

"What trouble did you get into?" Eddy asked.

"Is that why you were stealing?"

"I'm not admitting to anything about that. The truth is I got into gambling. I thought if I could win enough money then I could change my life. But all I did was lose, over and over." She wiped her eyes again and then looked up at the ceiling. "Vince warned me not to get in too deep, but I just kept getting in deeper."

"That's when Maury got involved?" Samantha frowned.

"Yes, I went to him for a loan to cover my debt. I was really struggling. I knew that I had a problem. Maury gave me the loan, but then he started acting like he owned me. I was scared of what he might try to make me do. I was under scrutiny here, and I had no money, so I turned to Vince. He understood. He helped me," she said with despair. "He told me that it was my chance to get things right, and that I should pay everything off and start with a clean slate." Her chin trembled with grief. "He wanted me to have the chance he never did."

"Sounds like he was looking out for you." Samantha smiled sympathetically.

"He was." Lily nodded. "The funny thing is, I broke up with him because I didn't like what he was involved in. Then I ended up getting into illegal things, too."

"What do you mean, what he was involved in?" Eddy asked. His eyes narrowed as he sensed she was about to provide information that they needed to hear.

Lily pursed her lips. She looked thoughtful for a moment. "It doesn't matter now, does it?" She looked from Eddy to Samantha. "He's gone, so why does it matter?"

"It matters because right now there is a man in jail, Simon, who did not kill Vince," Samantha spoke in a firm tone and locked eyes with Lily. "You know that he did not do it."

"Simon wouldn't hurt anyone." Lily cast her eyes towards the desk and sighed. "But I don't know who killed Vince. Dragging his name through the mud isn't going to change that."

"Who are you scared of, Lily?" Eddy abruptly asked. His tone was stern but almost paternal. "Who has you frightened enough that you would let someone who cared about you go to the grave without justice?"

Lily met Eddy's eyes with tears shadowing her own. "People like us don't care about justice, Eddy. We know that it doesn't exist. Vince was involved with some very dangerous people. He wouldn't want anyone else to pay for his mistakes. So no, I'm not going to name any names, and you're damn right, I'm scared. You two have no idea what you've gotten yourselves into. I suggest you stop looking into this before you both end up just like Vince."

Eddy narrowed his eyes. He looked over at Samantha. Samantha nodded a little.

"I'm sorry for your loss, Lily," Samantha murmured. "If you think of anything else that you might want to tell us, just let us know."

As soon as they were out of the office Eddy turned to look at Samantha. "Do you think she's telling the truth? A gambling addict will do almost anything to get their next fix."

"I do think that she's telling the truth. I don't think that grief like that can be faked." She sighed. "But I'm not always the best judge. Why didn't you wait for me?"

"I thought you weren't coming." He shrugged. "I didn't want her getting away without talking to her."

"I understand," Samantha acknowledged. "I just couldn't sleep last night. I was worried about so many things. Then when the sun came up I fell asleep for a little while."

"It's not good that you're not sleeping, Samantha," he spoke quietly as he turned to look at her. "Maybe this is all too much for you? Why don't you let Walt and me handle it for a while?"

"I don't think so." Samantha laughed. "I'm not going to wait for someone to tell me that everything is fine. I want to be involved. I just don't know where to start now. Do you?"

"I think we need to take a short break from the case. We need to come back at it with a fresh mind. There is something in all of this mess that makes sense, that makes a connection. We just have to be able to see clearly to find it." He glanced towards the parking lot. "I'm going to go for a drive. Why don't you get some sleep? Then we can meet at Walt's to discuss things. He is another set of eyes that can help sort through everything."

"All right." Samantha nodded. She was tempted to ask to join him for the drive, but she knew that he needed some quiet time to think. As she turned to walk back towards her villa she yawned. She really did need some sleep. She thought about Simon as she walked past a beautiful garden that he tended. It was still as bright and cheerful as ever, but Samantha knew that wouldn't last long. Without Simon's touch, the flowers would begin to fade. She unlocked the door of her villa, but before she could open her door, she heard someone calling her name. Samantha turned to see Jo walking up to her.

"How are you?" Jo asked.

"Not too great." Samantha yawned again. "I didn't get much sleep last night."

"I just wanted to check on you. How is the case progressing?" Jo pretended to just be asking casual questions, but Samantha could tell that she was genuinely curious which surprised Samantha because Jo seemed so adamant that she stay out of the case.

"We've hit some roadblocks," Samantha acknowledged. "It's more complicated than we expected."

"Well, I'll poke around a bit, and see if there's anything I can turn up," Jo offered. Samantha thought about what Lily had said about the danger they were all in.

"If you do, Jo, be careful. We're not entirely sure what we're dealing with." Samantha shuddered. "Whoever did this was pretty ruthless."

"I'll be careful," Jo said. "I'll let you know if I

139

find anything. Try to get some rest."

"Thanks Jo." Samantha let herself into her villa and then closed the door. It meant a lot that Jo had come to check on her. She just hoped that she wasn't pulling Jo into something too dangerous.

Chapter Ten

After a short nap, Samantha woke to the sun setting. She blinked a few times as she tried to figure out why she was waking up at twilight. Then everything came rushing back to her. She sat up and yawned. She was still pretty tired, but she was curious about what Walt and Eddy might have found.

Samantha was lost in thought as she walked along the path towards Walt's villa. In the past she would have been on full alert while walking alone in the dark. Since she had become accustomed to the security of Sage Gardens she had begun to let her guard down. Now and then she felt an urge to protect herself, but most of the time she felt as if she was walking through her own backyard.

When Samantha noticed something out of the corner of her eye, she dismissed it at first as palm fronds brushing across the side of a villa. A moment later it registered that the shadows she had seen had a distinctively human shape. She felt uneasy as she thought of the possibilities. Despite the fact that Sage Gardens was a gated community there was always the risk of someone breaking in. There hadn't been any recent break-ins, but with the laid back nature of most of the residents, they might be viewed as easy targets.

Samantha decided to double back and check. Her mind filled with images of what might happen to her if she was in her villa alone and someone broke in. She would hope that someone walking by would notice. She knew that the villa belonged to a much older gentleman by the name of Bill. He was getting weaker in his old age and required a bit more attention than most of the residents. Samantha reasoned that perhaps one of his nurses was responsible for the shadows that she had seen. But there was always the possibility that was not the case.

As she walked up towards the villa, she heard a scuffling sound from inside. Her heart froze. It felt as if it refused to beat. Fear coursed through her as the door burst open and two men rushed out past her. She could only tell that they were men, and nothing else about them, as they wore long, dark clothing and thick, black masks. Samantha jumped back as they blazed past her. Her heart began pounding again, hard. The door to the villa was still hanging slightly open. She fumbled for her phone. As she pulled it out of her purse she poked her head inside the villa. It was very dark.

"Hello?" Her voice carried through the shadows. "Is anyone home?"

She received no answer. She dialed Eddy's number. He answered on the first ring.

"Samantha?"

"Eddy, I think Bill Green's villa just got broken into."

"What? Are the police there?" Eddy asked.

"No, I called you first. The men who broke in are gone."

"What's going on here?" The voice drifted from behind Samantha. She turned to find Bill standing a few feet away.

"Bill! I'm so glad that you're okay." She sighed with relief.

"I'll be right there." Eddy hung up the phone. Samantha tucked her phone back into her purse.

"Of course I'm okay. I just went to the late buffet. What are you doing here, Samantha? Why is my door open?" He moved past her to look more closely at the door.

"I was walking by and I saw some movement around your villa. I came to check it out and two men ran out! We need to call the police." Samantha started to reach for her phone again. She was feeling so flustered that she couldn't figure out what she should do next.

"No, no police," Bill said sternly.

"Why no police?" Eddy asked. He walked up to the pair at a brisk pace.

"Look, I just don't want the trouble. There's nothing in my villa that anyone would want. I have an old television, a broken DVD player and an assortment of coffee mugs. Nothing worth any money. I'll take a look around, but I'm sure they realized there was nothing of value inside."

"Let me go in with you." Eddy walked up to the door with him.

"Be careful," Samantha spoke with concern.

As the two men disappeared into the villa, Samantha looked around the outside. She was searching for some sign of how the two men had broken in. She knew that she had seen their shadows on the outside of the villa when she was walking up. That meant they must have gotten inside rather quickly. She did not find any open windows or other signs of a break-in. When she walked back around the other side of the house Eddy and Bill were stepping back outside.

"It doesn't look like anything was taken." Eddy frowned.

"Why would someone break in and not take anything?" Samantha asked.

"Maybe you scared them off," Eddy replied.

He glanced over his shoulder at the villa. "They probably saw you coming and decided to get out before you could catch them."

"But how did they get in?" Samantha wondered. "None of the windows are broken. Bill, did you leave your door unlocked?"

"Never. I always lock up," Bill said with confidence. Samantha knew that he might have forgotten, everyone had at some point. But what were the chances that on the one night Bill forgot to lock up, someone broke in?

"Did anyone else have a key? Or did you hide one somewhere?" Samantha looked at the doormat.

"No, I've got the only one," Bill sounded impatient. "Listen, no one took anything. I'm not worried about it. I just want to get to bed."

"What about the police?" Eddy locked eyes with him. "Don't you think that you should file a report?"

"Of what? Someone breaking into my house

and finding nothing to steal?" Bill laughed a little. "Thanks, but I think I'll skip that humiliation. No, what I'd like to do is just forget it happened. Either it was some kids up to no good, or someone broke into the wrong house. I don't want any trouble and now they know there's nothing to steal they won't be back."

"You really should think about filing a report." Samantha frowned as Eddy steered her away from the door.

"We can't force him," he said quietly. "If he doesn't want to make a report he doesn't have to."

"They weren't kids, Eddy." Samantha looked back at Bill to plead with him again, but he had already closed his door.

"It's a good thing you scared them off. If you hadn't Bill might have walked right into the robbery, and that doesn't always end well." Eddy gestured to the sidewalk, "I'll walk you to your villa."

Samantha nodded silently. As they walked her mind was churning. She kept replaying the sight of the two men pushing past her. Had they been armed? She didn't remember seeing any weapons. They didn't seem to be carrying anything.

"First a murder, and now a break-in," Samantha commented sadly. "I'm starting to think that Sage Gardens isn't that safe after all."

"Nowhere is safe," Eddy said grimly. "Not really. We buy into the idea of security, but walls and guards will never stop a determined criminal."

"But Bill said he had nothing of value for anyone to steal. Why would a criminal be determined to get into his villa?" Samantha questioned as they reached her villa. "Something just doesn't feel right about it, Eddy."

"I think you're right." Eddy nodded. "I'll look into whether there have been any other reports of break-ins in the area, first thing in the morning. Let's not go to Walt's tonight. He said he was looking into a few things himself. I think it's better if the three of us keep a low profile right now. Just make sure you lock up tight, all right?"

"Eddy, are you worried about me?" Samantha smiled sweetly.

"All right, enough of that, just make sure you lock up," Eddy grumbled gruffly under his breath and walked away. Samantha watched him go with an amused smile. It always left Eddy flustered when she called him out on how warm and kind he could be. He seemed to prefer to project the image of a tough guy. But she had learned over the course of their friendship that it was just a show.

Samantha stepped inside and did take extra care to make sure all the windows and doors were locked in her villa. Even though she knew she was secure when she lay down in bed she had a hard time falling asleep. She kept having flashbacks to the two men rushing out of Bill's villa. She had been so frightened by their sudden appearance. Briefly, so briefly that she hadn't even realized it at the time, she had wondered if they would kill her. She still had quite a few fears buried deep within her, and the two men had certainly awakened one of them.

It made her angry to think that she could be doing something as simple as walking home, and two criminals had managed to steal her sense of safety. It made her angrier when she thought about what might have happened if Bill had walked in on them. It wasn't as if she couldn't hold her own in a fight, at least she liked to tell herself she could. But what about the older or handicapped residents that would barely be able to defend themselves? They counted on Sage Gardens to be a safe place where they could enjoy their retirement. She wasn't going to let two criminals ruin that sense of security for her friends and neighbors. By the time the sun rose she was determined to go back to Bill and have another conversation with him about filing a police report.

Chapter Eleven

At first light Samantha was up and in the shower. She was out the door as soon as she was dressed. She knew just where to find the person she was looking for. Walt was awake and sipping his tea on his front porch as usual.

"Morning, Samantha. You're up early. Would you like some tea?" Walt stood up from his chair. Samantha climbed the steps onto his porch.

"Walt, I need your help." She met his eyes with a determined look.

"At your service." Walt smiled warmly.

"I want you to come with me to talk to Bill Green. I caught two men breaking into his villa last night and he refuses to file a police report. I want to have another conversation with him about that. Eddy is busy with his police contacts this morning. Bill is a little old fashioned and I just think that he would listen to you." Samantha took a breath and shook her head. "He has to file a police report."

"Oh, well." Walt frowned. "Isn't that really his choice, Samantha?"

"It is, but I want him to think about the other residents that could be at risk. These men need to be caught," Samantha said sternly.

"All right, all right. Don't get too worked up." Walt picked up his jacket. "I'll go with you. But you can't force people to do the things you want them to, Samantha. Bill may be of the philosophy of not wanting to ruffle feathers."

"I can't imagine how anyone could just be okay with someone breaking into their home." Samantha sighed. "I just want to talk to him about how much of an impact it will have if he files a police report. That way Sage Gardens can amp up the security at night."

"As if they haven't after what happened to Vince?" Walt pointed out. They began walking across the courtyard towards Bill's villa.

"No, they believe they've caught the killer.

That means they will start to relax again." Samantha grimaced with concern.

"You don't believe that they caught the killer, do you?" Walt asked quietly.

"I don't, no." Samantha shook her head. "I don't think that Simon is a killer. And like Eddy pointed out, his feet are way too big to have made those footprints."

"But those footprints might have nothing to do with the crime," Walt reminded her gently. "It's important to keep an open mind."

"I guess." Samantha paused in front of Bill's villa. "I think I'll feel better if I just check with Bill and make sure that he knows he has a right to protect himself."

"Fair enough." Walt nodded. The two walked up to the door of the villa. Samantha started to knock, but before she could the door swung open. Bill stood there in his thin, blue plaid boxers and sleeveless undershirt. Samantha gulped at the sight of his curly, gray chest hair.

"What the heck?" Bill fumed. "Samantha, will you please get off my newspaper!"

Samantha stepped back and realized that she had been standing on Bill's newspaper.

"Bill, can we talk to you for a moment?" Walt asked. Samantha was still trying to recover from the shock of seeing Bill nearly naked.

"What is this about?" Bill picked up his newspaper and shook it off with an annoyed frown.

"I think we need to talk about what happened last night a little more," Samantha pleaded.

"Really, you need to stop harping on about it." Bill scowled as he looked at Samantha. "I don't know if you're trying to create some kind of drama for yourself, but me, I want none of it."

"It's nothing like that," Samantha insisted. "I just want to talk about the men I saw coming out of your house. They had to be in there for a reason. If we let the police have a look, we might be able to find out why."

"No police," Bill said staunchly. "I've had enough of them in my lifetime. They never caused me anything but trouble. If I want to have my peace, I should be allowed to have it. Whoever it was that you claimed to have seen didn't steal or break anything. So, I really don't care."

"And if they come back?" Walt asked. "What are you going to do to protect yourself?"

Bill lowered his eyes nervously. It was clear that he felt vulnerable. Samantha thought perhaps that was why he was so against reporting the break-in. Maybe he was afraid that the criminals would seek revenge and he would have no way to defend himself.

"Look, I'm sure it was just a mistake. What could I possibly have that they would want?" Bill looked perplexed. "There's nothing."

"There has to be something." Walt gazed past Bill. "May we come in and take a look around? We're not the police."

"Well, all right. I suppose." Bill nodded. He allowed them to move past him into the villa.

"Let me just get some pants." He headed off to the bedroom. While he was gone Walt swept his gaze over every detail of the living room, dining room, and kitchen. Samantha could see him processing everything he was seeing as if he was some kind of human computer.

She remained silent as he worked as she did not want to disturb him. Samantha took the time to look around as well. She had been so shaken the night before that it was hard for her to focus. Now that she was thinking more clearly she could see that Bill had been right. His electronics were all older and his furniture was shabby. There was nothing within view of the windows that would be perceived as valuable. So why had the men broken in? Samantha narrowed her eyes as she wondered what she was missing.

"Aha!" Walt smiled victoriously.

"What is it? What do you see?" Samantha looked around for what he might have noticed.

"Take a look." Walt gestured to the table. Samantha looked at the table. There was nothing on it other than the paper that Bill had just picked up.

"I don't understand." She peered more closely at the table.

"Look at the carpet." Walt pointed towards the place where the table legs met the carpet.

"Oh, there are indentations beside the legs," Samantha murmured.

"Which means that someone has recently moved this table." Walt knocked lightly on the solid wood piece of furniture. "Do you think that Bill would be able to move this on his own?"

"Move that table?" Bill asked. He walked back into the room, luckily this time with pants on. "I haven't moved it since I moved in. I doubt I could budge it."

"If you didn't move it, then who did?" Samantha asked. "And why?" She eyed the carpet closely in search of any seams that might be showing. "Perhaps there's a hidden compartment?"

"Have you had anyone else in the house in the past few days?" Walt asked as Bill looked at the table strangely.

"Only Jacob, the maintenance worker. He came in to take a look at my garbage disposal earlier this week. But no one else." He scratched the back of his head. "I'm not sure why anyone would want to move that table. There's nothing hidden as far as I know."

"Not under the table, above." Walt pointed up to the ceiling. "See those marks?"

There was a scattering of dark marks on the ceiling around the attic entrance. The table was positioned perfectly so that someone standing on top of the table might be able to open the attic access.

"Did Jacob have any reason to go in the attic?" Samantha asked Bill.

"No, not that I know of, he was only here to work on the garbage disposal. Do you think that whatever the men were looking for is up there?" Bill asked nervously. "What do you think it might be?"

"There's only one way to find out." Samantha looked up at the ceiling. "We'll have to go in."

"I certainly will not." Walt was adamant. "It's going to be filthy in there."

"I would, but my hip." Bill patted his right hip. Samantha eyed the opening. In the past she might have been spry enough to make it through, but now with a little more weight around her belly and her hips spreading there was no way she was going to squeeze through the attic door.

"I can't fit. But I know someone who can." Samantha smiled. After all Jo had offered to help look around.

Samantha pulled out her cell phone. She dialed Jo's number.

"Hi Samantha," Jo answered with a hint of impatience. "I was just going to head into town. What do you need?"

"Do you have a few minutes? I could use your help with something." Samantha braced herself for Jo's avoidance.

"Depends on what it is."

"I need you to get into a small space for me. No one else will fit. What do you say?" Samantha asked hopefully.

"Samantha, I'm not your personal cat burglar you know." Jo laughed a little. "It has to be right now?"

"It is pretty time sensitive. We're at villa 21." Samantha felt a bit guilty. She knew that Jo was right about her often asking for her expertise.

"All right, I'll be there in a few." Jo hung up without another word. Samantha was surprised that she agreed so easily. She hung up her phone and turned to face Walt.

"Jo's going to be here in a couple of minutes to help us out."

"Why did you call her?" Walt asked. He looked a little tense. He was always a little uncomfortable around Jo because of her past.

"Trust me, she is the best person for the job."

Samantha looked over at Bill. "She'll see what's up in the attic."

"Don't you think we should call the police about this?" Walt asked.

"No police," Bill repeated. "I don't care who crawls around in the attic, but unless we find a dead body up there, no police."

"Oh, I didn't even consider that," Walt said with concern. "What if there is a body up there?"

"I don't know. I don't think that anyone would go to all the trouble of hoisting a body up into the ceiling. Besides, even if it's hidden, it would begin to smell," Samantha pointed out. "No, I think it must be something fairly small."

"I just don't understand why they would hide anything here." Bill frowned. "I'm not involved with any kind of criminal. Why would they use my villa?"

"Probably because it's the last place that someone would look," Walt suggested. "It makes sense. You have no connection with the criminals.

Plus, it may have been just a matter of opportunity."

A moment later there was a knock on the door. Bill looked at Samantha and Walt. "Should I answer it?" he asked.

"Go ahead, it should be Jo." Samantha nodded. Still, when Bill walked towards the door she watched him with some apprehension. She wasn't sure it would be Jo. The case of who killed Vince was unfolding in very strange ways. She had no idea what to expect. Bill hesitantly opened the door.

"Oh, hello," his voice became soft and warm. Samantha grinned. She was sure it was Jo. The only two men she'd seen not trip all over themselves at the sight of her were Walt and Eddy. Samantha suspected they were just better at hiding it.

"Hi, is Samantha here?" Jo asked.

"She is, come in." Bill pushed open the door for her. Jo stepped inside. Samantha could see that she was mildly annoyed at being there in the first place.

"How can I help?" Jo asked.

"Last night I saw two men sneaking out of Bill's villa. We suspect that they were in here to hide something or maybe take back what they had hidden. We need your help to check it out."

"Okay, where did they hide it?" she asked.

Samantha pointed up at the entrance to the attic. "We think it's in there."

"And you have no idea what it might be?" Jo frowned.

"No clue." Samantha sighed. "It could really be anything, or even nothing."

Jo looked up at the ceiling with some hesitation. She glanced over at Walt who was standing nervously beside the table. "Shouldn't a gentleman be the one to do this?"

"No way!" Walt shuddered at the very thought. "Do you have any idea how dirty it will be up there? The dust, the grime..."

"Okay, okay. I don't really want to hear any

more about it!" Jo exclaimed and looked over at Samantha. "Aren't you supposed to be the brave one? Didn't you crawl through tight spaces when investigating stories?"

"I did, as in, in the past," Samantha recalled. "I'm afraid if I tried to wriggle my way through there I might get stuck."

"Listen, how long is this going to take?" Bill asked. He tapped his foot impatiently. "I have a lunch date with a friend of mine."

"Sorry, just a few minutes." Samantha smiled at him to reassure him. Jo looked up at the attic door again.

"It shouldn't take me long. But if there are bats, there will be consequences." She looked directly at Samantha with a fierce glare.

"Understood." Samantha nodded.

"Okay, let's see what's hiding up there," Jo muttered. She jumped up onto the table as if her feet were made of springs. With ease she opened the attic door and slid it to the side inside the attic.

She grabbed the sides of the opening.

"Do you need a boost?" Samantha offered. She grabbed Jo's legs at the thighs.

"Ugh! No!" Jo snapped. She shook Samantha's hands off her. With a slight tug she lifted herself up into the attic through sheer upper arm strength. Samantha stared in wonder at the athletic woman. She couldn't imagine doing a single chin up let alone swinging her entire body up into the attic. Once Jo was inside she coughed a few times.

"Yes, there is plenty of dust," she called down.

"Anything else?" Samantha asked with some urgency in her voice. "Do you see drugs? Or weapons?"

"What?" Bill gasped. "What do you think is up there? It's not a bomb is it?" His eyes grew wide with fear.

"I'm sure it's not a bomb," Samantha spoke kindly.

"Actually, there is a chance it could be." Walt

165

cleared his throat. "Statistically speaking."

"Walt!" Samantha growled at him. Walt gulped and lowered his eyes.

"Relax, no guns, no weapons, no bombs," Jo's muffled voice called out.

"So, there's nothing up there?" Samantha frowned. "Maybe they got what they came for after all."

"I don't think so!" Jo called out gleefully. She tossed something down through the opening of the attic entrance. The big green sack landed on the table below the attic with a thump. When it struck the table a plume of dust flew up into the air, covering Walt with a thin layer of it.

"Oh no!" Walt gulped, then he sealed his mouth tight and covered his nose. His other hand fluttered in a panic at his skin and clothes in an attempt to get rid of the dust that had gathered there.

Samantha grimaced and reached out to help him dust off his clothes. "You have to breathe,

Walt," she said. Walt's face was beginning to redden from holding his breath. Walt rushed out of the villa to get some fresh air.

"What is it?" Bill asked. Before Samantha could look inside the bag two more were tossed down from the ceiling. By the time the dust had settled, Jo had jumped down as well. Samantha looked up at her standing on the table. She expected the woman to be a mess from crawling around in the dust. Instead, her thick, dark hair was shimmering except for a few speckles of dust, her skin was smooth as ever, and she had a smug smile on her lips. Samantha was fascinated by Jo's ability to always look good no matter the circumstances.

"Look what I found!" Jo spoke proudly. She put one black boot on the top of one of the bags. "Let's discuss finder's fees."

"What is it?" Samantha asked. She pulled back the flap of one of the bags. What greeted her was the largest amount of money she had ever seen in her life. The other two bags were filled with just as much money. Samantha was absolutely stunned.

"Where did all of this come from?" she wondered out loud.

"That was in my attic?" Bill asked. "Does that make it mine?"

"Oh no, it's mine," happiness coated Jo's voice. "I think I am going to buy my own island."

"It isn't anyone's!" Samantha said sharply. "We need to find out who it belongs to."

"You can't be seriously considering turning it into the police, Samantha," Jo said. She glared at Samantha. "There is no reason to even think about doing that."

"It's the only thing we can do," Walt said. He had inched his way back into the villa. He had found a napkin and held it over his nose and mouth to keep out the dust that still lingered in the air. "That money is illegal, there's no question about it. Who it belongs to, and how it was earned, those are things we'll have to figure out. But there's no way anyone earns that much money legally and then hides it in a ceiling. Is there Jo?" He locked eyes with the woman who was still perched on top of the table.

"All the police will do is put it in lock up," Jo protested. "This is free money. It belongs to criminals, they shouldn't get it back. Why should the police have it?"

"Uh, excuse me." Bill raised his hand. He was intimidated by the glares that Walt and Jo were exchanging.

"Yes, Bill?" Samantha asked. She was relieved at the interruption. From the way Jo was looking at Walt she was expecting the woman to sprout claws at any time.

"I think we need to be careful about this," Bill spoke up. "I mean, obviously the two men who broke into my villa were looking for this money. They either didn't find it, or you interrupted them before they could, Samantha. So, if we give the money to the police, they will know that the money has been found. Then they might come back for revenge."

"He makes a good point." Walt looked at Jo grimly. "Criminals can always be counted on to make rash emotional decisions."

Jo scrunched up her nose. She leaned closer to Walt. Then she gave her long hair a sharp whip. The hair didn't come near Walt, but whipping it caused all of the dust that had been clinging to it to spray off the thick strands. Walt received a face full of dust.

"Jo!" Samantha admonished.

"What?" Jo asked with an innocent smile. "I was just trying to get some dust out of my hair. It gets itchy." She playfully scratched at her head. Walt had fled the villa again for fresh air. Samantha sighed. She found herself wishing that Eddy was there. For all of his gruff nature he was good at taking charge and keeping things from getting too chaotic.

"Okay, let's all take a breath," Samantha did her best to keep her voice calm. "We don't need to make any quick decisions. Right now we know what the criminals were looking for. Knowing who and why is important, because like Bill said, they're not going to quit trying to get this money. They will be back to try to retrieve it, and they might be violent this time."

"That's very possible." Jo nodded solemnly.

"Wait a minute." Samantha snapped her fingers. "We do have one clue. How the criminals got inside the villa in the first place."

"What do you mean?" Walt asked.

"I mean, they didn't break in. Bill claims everything was locked up. So, how did they get in?" Samantha pointed to the front door. "There's no evidence of any damage to the door."

"You think they had a key?" Jo suggested.

"Yes. I think maybe they did. Bill, does anyone have a spare key to your villa?" Samantha asked.

"No. No spares. I mean if I ever get locked out, the office always has a spare." He shrugged.

"Ah, I see," Samantha said.

Walt met her eyes. "Which brings us back to

Lily."

Samantha nodded slowly. She didn't want to believe it, but Lily had quite a large sum of money when she paid Maury. Was it possible that she had been paid off to somehow take Vince out? She really hoped that wasn't the case, but she couldn't be sure.

Chapter Twelve

Eddy walked into the police station cautiously. He watched for any sign of Detective Brunner. He knew that if he was caught again, he would be in some serious trouble. He didn't relish the idea of ending up in handcuffs. However, Detective Brunner didn't seem to be there. Eddy walked carefully towards the lab. He could see Chris through the window, leaning over his computer. He hoped that Chris would still be willing to help him after the lashing that Detective Brunner had likely given him.

A few of the officers noticed him as he walked towards the lab, but only gave him a slight nod of respect. The veteran officers knew Eddy or at least knew of him and never gave him a hard time. Once he reached the lab Eddy knocked lightly on the door. Chris spun around on his computer chair. When he saw Eddy through the window he grimaced. Then he stood up from the chair. He walked over and opened the door.

"Eddy, you shouldn't be here," he warned him.

"I know that. But I'm here." Eddy offered a charming smile.

"I don't want to see what happens if Detective Brunner spots you." Chris looked very worried.

"Then we should make this quick. I need to know if there were any break-ins recently in the area around Sage Gardens." Eddy leaned back against the table and waited for Chris to look up the information. As Chris' fingers flew over the keys he spoke to Eddy.

"I don't know what you're getting yourself involved in, Eddy, but you should know that Detective Brunner isn't flexible. He's one of those by the book types."

"Maybe, if he were more by the book this murder would be solved." Eddy cast a glance grimly through the windowed door.

"He's not a bad detective. But there's a lot of pressure right now to close cases as soon as they open." Chris shook his head. "I'm not seeing a single reported break-in in the past six months within ten miles of Sage Gardens. Do you want me to go further out?"

"No, that's fine. I thought we might be barking up the wrong tree, anyway." He sighed. "I'm not sure which tree to be focusing on to be honest."

"Well, I think you better consider disappearing, because Detective Brunner just stepped off the elevator. Use the side door." Chris pointed to the door on the other side of the lab. "You should be able to get out without being seen."

Eddy nodded and headed straight for the door. The last thing he needed was a run-in with Detective Brunner.

On his way back to Sage Gardens, Eddy sent a text to Samantha. He wanted to discuss the case as soon as they could.

Samantha, meet me at my villa please.

Samantha read over the text. It didn't offer any more information. She knew that if Eddy had texted her there was a good reason. He was not one for using technology for fun. She hurried across the courtyard towards Eddy's villa which wasn't very far from her own. As she neared it she noticed Jacob, a maintenance worker for Sage Gardens. He was replacing one of the light bulbs in the street lights that lined the pavement that led down to the water. Samantha was glad to see that he was doing it, as she hated to walk down near the water when the lights weren't working.

As Samantha walked past him he reached up and adjusted his cap. Something about his cap made Samantha's mind come alive with warning bells. It took her a moment to figure it out. Finally, she registered that the ratty cap had the exact same emblem on the front of the cap which was inside the backpack that she had found in the water. This made her breath catch in her chest.

Was it possible that she had just walked past a murderer? She took a breath and tried to calm herself down. Just because Jacob was wearing the same type of cap, that didn't mean that he was the killer. Maybe the backpack had nothing to do with the murder anyway. There were likely hundreds of those caps in the area. There was no way to be sure that it was the same one. But it made her skin crawl just the same.

Samantha made her way down the sidewalk to Eddy's villa. When she knocked on the door, Walt opened it. She blinked a moment and wondered if she had gone to the wrong villa.

"Eddy called me." Walt held the door open for her.

"You will not believe what I just saw," Samantha's voice trembled with a mixture of fear and excitement.

"What?" Eddy asked as he sat down at his dining room table. Samantha noticed that his expression looked very grim. It was clear that whatever he had found out that morning had not been good.

"Jacob, the maintenance worker, was wearing the same cap that was inside the backpack." Samantha sat down beside him. Walt joined them as well. "Do you know what this means?"

"You think that Jacob is the killer?" Eddy said dubiously.

"He seems like a nice enough fellow," Walt offered.

"So did Vince, but he was obviously involved in something that he shouldn't have been," Samantha remarked. "I just think it can't be a coincidence that it was the same cap."

"Are you sure that it was the same cap?" Walt asked. "You only saw it briefly. Is it possible that you have them mixed up?"

"I don't think so." Samantha closed her eyes for a moment and recalled the cap she had seen. "No, it was the same one. I know it was."

"So, what does that tell us?" Eddy sat back in his chair. "Either Jacob just happens to have the same cap, or the backpack belonged to him, or he stole the backpack and the drugs and kept the cap. None of those things actually make him a killer."

"Did you tell Eddy about the money?" Samantha asked Walt.

"I did." Walt nodded. "He agrees with me that we should turn it into the police."

"Just a minute. We haven't figured out how the two men got into Bill's house last night. But if it was Jacob he would have access to the spare keys in the office to make repairs. That means he could have been the one to hide the money, and to try to get it back."

"She's right." Walt rapped his knuckles against the table. "It makes sense that he would be able to move around undetected. He could have been watching to see when Bill left for the buffet."

"That does make sense," Eddy said thoughtfully. "The only problem is that we have no real proof. We can't prove that Jacob was in Bill's house, let alone that he was involved with a murder, based on a cap."

"What we do have is the chance to set a trap," Samantha's voice rose with a hint of excitement.

"What do you mean?" Walt looked at her warily.

"I mean that if Jacob thinks that money is still in Bill's attic, he's going to try to steal it again. We could have Bill make sure that Jacob overhears that he is going out, and then we could wait for Jacob to break in. If we catch him trying to get the money, it will be clear that he's involved."

"I don't know," Walt muttered. "That sounds rather dangerous."

"It sounds like a sting." Eddy rubbed his hand along his cheek. "It might just work. But I think we need to connect the dots first. So, Jacob might be involved, but how was he connected to Vince?"

"I can do a little research on Vince to see if he has any connections to Jacob. But we need to hurry if we're going to do anything. We can't just wait and give Jacob time to disappear." Samantha shivered as she remembered being alone with Jacob once before beside the tall grass where Vince's body had been found. It made her anxious to think that she might have been that vulnerable around a killer.

"All right, Samantha, you see what you can find out. Walt, look into the finances and see if you can figure anything out on that end. I'll check in with my contacts regarding Jacob. We're getting close now, I can feel it."

Samantha nodded at Eddy. "For Simon's sake, I hope you're right."

Chapter Thirteen

As the three friends went their separate ways, Samantha kept an eye out for Jacob. She hoped that she hadn't done anything to tip him off that she was onto him. She hesitated outside the door of her villa. Instead of just unlocking the door as she usually did she stood back a few feet and searched for anything that might be out of place.

Since everything seemed to be in order she finally stepped forward and unlocked her door. She eased it slowly open and peeked inside. She checked for anything that looked out of the ordinary before stepping in. Nothing seemed to be disturbed. She locked the door behind her. Samantha was still nervous as she walked into her office and sat down at her computer. She was looking forward to a time when the murder was solved and she could relax.

She laid her fingertips on the keys. She knew what she wanted to research but her mind drifted back to Vince. She thought of the man who had often been a daily part of her life, and yet she barely knew who he was. She wondered how life could get like that, with people remaining strangers despite daily interaction. That was the task ahead of her. Who was Vince? How was he linked to Jacob? Was there any connection at all.

One trick that Samantha had learned during her years of doing research for stories was to follow the forwarding addresses, and the family. First she looked up Vince's immediate family members. His parents were deceased many years earlier. He had one brother and one sister. The sister lived across the country which made her an unlikely source for a connection, but not completely off the table. It was possible that Jacob was an old boyfriend or husband of hers. As Samantha followed the trails between the siblings, and Jacob, she found no connection between Jacob and Vince. Despite the fact that they were both at Sage Gardens at the same time many days, there was no evidence that either of them spent any time together outside of work.

Once she began looking into Vince's brother, Carl, she started to feel she might be getting somewhere. He had lived in some of the same towns as Jacob. In fact at one point Carl and Jacob had lived in the same apartment complex. Samantha dug a little deeper and found that they had lived there at the same time. She also checked on the crime rates for the complex and found that there had been a heavy problem with drugs at the time. It made sense to her that Carl and Jacob could have gotten to know each other while living in the complex. Maybe Carl had connected Jacob with his brother, Vince. Or maybe there had been some bad blood between Carl and Jacob.

Maybe Vince had started trouble in an attempt to settle the score. Samantha now knew how the two men were connected. What she didn't know was whether the relationship between them was one of friendship or business. She sat back from the computer and smiled to herself. There was one way she thought she could find out exactly how Vince and Jacob got along. She picked up her phone and dialed the office.

"Hello?"

Samantha recognized the voice right away. It was the office assistant, Lily.

"Hi Lily, it's Samantha."

"Oh, hi Samantha," Lily sounded uncomfortable. She had good reason to be after Samantha and Eddy had pretty much interrogated her about her relationship with Vince. Samantha still suspected that Lily might have somehow been involved in the murder.

"I have a question that I hope that you can answer," Samantha said warmly.

"Oh, more questions." Lily cleared her throat. "Fine. What is it?"

"Jacob, the maintenance man. Is he a friend of Vince's?"

"Jacob? Why are you asking about him?" Lily asked grimly.

"I was just wondering if maybe you put in a good word to get Jacob his job here."

"Why would I have?" Lily asked.

"Because Jacob and Vince knew each other."

"Look, all I know is that one day Vince brought Jacob into the office to apply for the job. I didn't recommend anybody. But the manager liked Vince, and he hired Jacob on the spot because of it." Lily sighed. "I still can't believe he's gone."

Samantha felt a twinge of guilt for putting Lily through the difficult conversation. But she knew that guilt would be erased when she figured out the truth about who had killed Vince.

"What do you think of Jacob, Lily?" Samantha asked.

"I'd rather not say." Lily was beginning to get very short. "I need to go, Samantha, I have work to do. If you have any more questions for me, why don't you get the police to ask them?" With that she hung up the phone. Samantha grimaced. She knew that Lily was quite upset. The question was, why? Was she upset because Vince was dead, or because she was about to be caught? Samantha wasn't convinced that Lily wasn't still a suspect, though she hoped it wasn't true. After hanging up with Lily she placed a call to Walt.

"Okay Walt, I have some information for you. I want you to look into Jacob's financials, as well as Vince's, and Vince's brother, Carl's." Samantha looked over the information on her computer to make sure that she hadn't missed anything.

"Oh? Do you think his brother had something to do with this?" Walt asked.

"I think that we're missing something. Supposedly Vince is the one who got Jacob the job. So, if he did that, why would Jacob turn around and kill Vince? They were obviously friends, at least at one point. Maybe the financials will tell the truth." She frowned. "Something has to lead to the truth."

"Money always tells the truth," Walt spoke with confidence. "I'll get on it right now."

"I'm going to go speak with Jo. I think we're going to need her help."

"Good luck with that." Walt chuckled a little. "She doesn't seem to be in a very helpful mood."

"Well, maybe if you were a little kinder to her, Walt..."

"Samantha, I'm not sure why you insist on involving her. You know that you're just playing with fire, don't you? A woman like Jo, she doesn't have loyalty to anyone," his tone softened as if he was trying to be gentle.

"I don't agree with that," Samantha spoke sternly. "I might know a little bit more about her than you do, Walt."

"No matter what you know, statistically speaking..."

"I know, I know. Once a thief, always a thief."

"Precisely." Walt hung up the phone.

Samantha frowned and tucked her phone into her purse. Walt might be right, but sometimes to catch a criminal you had to be a criminal, or at least have some firsthand experience.

***

After hanging up the phone with Samantha, Walt logged into his computer. It only took a few minutes to track down Jacob's assets. Walt gasped as he saw that Jacob owned a large house, a very expensive car and a boat. Walt imagined that the drug dealing had bought him that, not a job in maintenance.

He then did a search on Vince. Vince was in a completely different financial position. He was in huge debt.

He then did a search on Carl, Vince's brother. He discovered that Carl and Vince's parents had been killed in a car accident when the brothers were young. No money had been left behind.

"So, they were orphans, along with their sister," Walt said softly. From his research he believed that Vince was in more debt than he could find proof of, probably illegal debt and it was not a surprise to Walt that the young man had ended up dead.

Chapter Fourteen

Eddy sorted through the papers he had spread out before him on the table. Although everything was on the computer, he did much better with hard copies. Each piece of paper had a list of the crimes that either Vince or Jacob had committed. He also found a history of crimes that Jacob and Vince's brother, Carl, committed together. It was really rather overwhelming to see that three men could cause such destruction and chaos. Their history of crime went back to their juvenile records. Eddy couldn't get the information from those, but he guessed it was more of the same.

There were arrests for assault, arrests for possession and distribution of drugs, as well as arrests for petty theft. He wondered how it came to be that the two men could even be hired with such records. But he understood that knowing the right person could make all the difference. As he swept all of the papers up into a pile there was a knock at his door. He looked up at it for a moment. His mind had been immersed in crime and for an instant he forgot that he was no longer an active police officer with a gun constantly on his hip. He brushed his palm along his side, instinctively looking for it. He shook himself out of the memory and walked over to the door. When he opened it he found Samantha standing outside.

"Sorry to just drop in." She offered an apologetic smile.

"You know you're always welcome, Sam." Eddy stepped back to allow her inside. Then he closed the door again.

"I was going to call to give you this information, but I was on my way to look for Jo, so I figured I'd stop by. I think there is a pretty strong connection between Jacob and Vince."

"I can see that, too." Eddy gestured to the pile of paper on his dining room table. "They have been arrested together more than once."

"So, it is likely that Jacob was involved in Vince's death. Maybe we'll be able to get Simon off the hook with this information," her voice started to rise with excitement.

"Well, that's not exactly true," Eddy muttered. "What we have is a connection, not a crime. So, Vince and Jacob knew each other. That doesn't mean that Jacob killed Vince. If they were friends why would he?"

"Okay, that is something that we don't know yet. But it seems they were working hand in hand. So, they both must have been involved in something dangerous." She frowned.

"Yes, which means that we are wading deeper and deeper into a dangerous situation," Eddy said grimly. "I think we need to slow down and think this through."

"Eddy, if we slow down then Jacob is likely to disappear. He is probably only still hanging around till he manages to get the money. Then he'll disappear," Samantha spoke with conviction. "We can't let that happen, Eddy. I wanted to see if Jo could break into the shed where Jacob keeps his stuff and see if there is something of Jacob's that can prove his guilt, then we might be able to get all of this settled quickly."

"Or she might get caught breaking in." Eddy shook his head. "I don't know about that."

"You said yourself that we needed more proof of Jacob's involvement." Samantha placed her hands on her hips. "How else do you think we're going to get any solid evidence? If the cops even question Jacob he'll probably destroy any evidence and disappear."

"That may be, but we can't just go around breaking into places, Samantha."

"We won't be. Jo will be. What are the chances that she won't be able to break into a simple garden shed, Eddy? She's broken into museums and mansions with the highest security. I think that she can handle a padlock." Samantha laughed a little.

"So, you're just going to run off and get Jo involved? What happens if it goes sideways, Samantha?" He locked eyes with her. "What do you think is going to happen to Jo?"

Samantha glanced away guiltily. She hadn't really thought about that. But she was still determined.

"It's her choice if she wants to take the risk. I'm sure she can handle it. There's nothing wrong with her using her skills to help rather than to hurt. I'll let you know when Jo and I find the evidence that we need." She turned and walked out of Eddy's villa.

Eddy contemplated going after her, but he decided against it. As she said, it was her choice if she wanted to take the risk.

He turned back into the villa just as his phone began to ring. He answered it quickly.

"Hello?" Eddy sounded a little annoyed.

"What's wrong? It's Walt," Walt said perplexed.

"I know it's you, Walt." It was clear that Eddy was exasperated. "What is it that you want?"

Walt narrowed his eyes. He thought about questioning Eddy further to figure out why he was annoyed, but he decided the information that he had to offer was more important.

"I did some research like Samantha asked me into the financial histories of Vince, his brother, and Jacob. I've found some interesting information."

"Ah yes, Samantha just left here. She was looking for Jo."

"Oh?"

"Yes, she is going to try to get Jo to break into the shed that Jacob stores his tools and personal items in," Eddy didn't sound terribly pleased about the idea.

"She does like to tap into Jo's..." he paused a moment, "creative talents."

"That she does," Eddy said sternly. "What did you find?"

"Jacob's assets are far too luxurious and expensive for a maintenance worker. He's either got his hands into something illegal, has a rich family, or he is very overpaid."

"Hmm, sounds like Samantha might be right then. She was determined that Jacob was the one who killed Vince."

"I think it's a very real possibility." Walt took a breath. "I noticed something else as well."

"What?"

"Vince was up to his ears in debt. For a young man, I'm not sure how he racked up so much debt in so little time. That is only the legal debt. He probably had more owed to loan sharks as well."

"Well, that is very telling." Eddy cleared his throat. "I suppose that if Vince was hurting for money he might have decided to increase his pay from Jacob, without letting Jacob in on the deal."

"Yes, I think that's very possible. Of course that's only what it looks like. It's possible that the funds were coming from somewhere else entirely."

"Sure, it's possible. Listen why don't you meet us down by the garden shed. If Samantha can convince Jo to break in, then we might be able to get even more evidence against Jacob."

Walt frowned. He considered leaving it at that, but he simply couldn't. "You don't have a problem with that, Eddy?"

"With what?"

"With encouraging Jo to fall back into old habits? If they are even old habits, for all we know she could still be an active criminal."

Eddy was silent for a moment. When he spoke again, his tone was lower than usual, "Listen Walt, not everything in life is as simple as right and wrong. I mean, technically when a police officer kicks down a door to stop a crime, he is breaking in. Only his crime is sanctioned. In this case, getting a search warrant for the garden shed will take time, and by the time it's done Jacob will likely be long gone. Is it right? I can't say for sure. But isn't it wrong to let a murderer go free?"

"But the old saying, two wrongs don't make a right," Walt reminded him.

"Of course. But two wrongs don't always make

another wrong either."

"Huh." Walt thought about arguing that point, but instead he nodded. "All right then. I'll meet you by the garden shed."

"See you there." Eddy hung up the phone.

Walt sat at his desk for a moment. He noticed that some of his pens were out of order. Carefully he eased them back into place. Walt was always happier when things had a place and an order. When it came to Jo, he didn't know where to put her. Was she a criminal? Was she reformed? He sighed and stood up from his chair. He was fairly certain that the debate raging in his mind was not one that was going to be settled any time soon.

Chapter Fifteen

Samantha knocked on Jo's door but there was no answer. She walked around the side of Jo's villa, hoping to peer in one of the windows. The villa looked completely empty inside. On a whim she walked around behind the villa. Samantha finally spotted Jo in her garden. It was a little surprising to her to see Jo in gardening gloves. The vivacious woman was not someone that struck Samantha as nurturing to plants.

"Jo, there you are," Samantha spoke as cheerfully as she could. "I've been trying to reach you."

"My phone is off for a reason." Jo pushed some dirt around a flower she had just planted. "I like to have some quiet when I work in the garden."

"I can understand that." Samantha smiled as she walked towards Jo, undeterred by the hint that she wanted to be alone. "I thought you might like an update on the case."

"No, I would not." Jo picked up a spade and began shifting soil.

"Really? It's getting very interesting." Samantha stood at the edge of the garden. She knew better than to get too close. Jo was still fairly volatile in Samantha's opinion.

"No, thank you. I prefer to stay out of the business of others. I find if I do that, then others pay me the same courtesy." She lifted her eyes to Samantha with an annoyed look. Samantha got the message plain and clear, but she pretended that she didn't. She wasn't going to give up that easily.

"I respect that. But you are already kind of involved, aren't you?" Samantha asked.

"What do you mean?" Jo studied her intently. She must have heard the conniving tone in Samantha's voice.

"I mean, I know what you did." Samantha cleared her throat. She took a slight step back from the garden, just in case Jo got the wild idea to attack her.

"I have no idea what you're talking about," Jo said. She spoke each word sharply.

"Maybe you can fool Eddy, and maybe even Walt, but not me, Jo. I saw you smuggle some of that money into your shirt before you left Bill's house," Samantha had lowered her voice, but apparently she still wasn't speaking quietly enough for Jo.

"Shh!" Jo hissed. She stood up quickly from the ground. "What are you playing at here, Samantha? Do you have any clue who you are dealing with?"

"I'm dealing with a woman whose skills I need to help me solve a murder." Samantha met Jo's eyes directly. Even as Jo prowled closer, Samantha stood her ground. She was doing her best to appear unafraid, but the truth was she was highly intimidated.

"I don't want to hear another word about it," Jo's voice was hard. "What happened was none of my business. I made the mistake of letting you convince me to get involved. What you're talking about is a serious crime. Not only murder, but also drugs. No one has that much cash hidden unless they are a major dealer. You think I'm afraid of the police finding out that I took some of that money, but that is not the case. The real people that you should be afraid of, are whoever that money belongs to, Samantha. Not me, not the police, but whoever that money belongs to. Because they will fight to the death to get it back. So no, I'm not getting in the middle of that mess. I've survived to this age, and I'm not going to blow my good track record now."

Samantha was stunned. She could actually see a glimmer of fear in Jo's eyes. She didn't think the woman was capable of being afraid. The fact that she was, made Samantha even more wary of what she might have gotten herself into.

"Jo, that's all the more reason to help us catch whoever did this. If they're behind bars, they can't hurt any of us." Samantha searched the other woman's eyes for some sign of compliance. She was certain that without Jo's help they would never find out the truth.

"Samantha, you're still wearing those rose-colored glasses. You don't get it, do you? The courts, the prisons, they are run by people who have their hands in every kind of crime. You're going to tell me that they are going to help us somehow? Protect us? No, that has never been the case for me." Jo shook her head. She turned back to her garden. "I'm not going to risk everything over a bus driver who had his hand too far in the cookie jar."

"What does that mean?" Samantha asked.

"Oh please. Drugs, money, and murder. There's only one reason a dealer ever risks his business to kill someone, and that's if they are a thief or a cop. I'm pretty sure our friendly tour guide wasn't a cop. So, that only leaves one option, doesn't it?" She glanced back over at Samantha. "This is how these people handle their business, Samantha, and your best bet is to just stay out of it."

"But it's too late for that now, isn't it?" Samantha asked. She felt a little breathless from Jo's description. "We are all involved."

Jo didn't answer. She just pushed more dirt around the flower. The poor, thin, green stem was nearly buried. Samantha knew that Jo was nervous.

"The truth is it's too late, isn't it, Jo? Maybe not for you, because you know how these things work. But it's too late for Walt, and me, and especially Eddy. Isn't it?" Samantha frowned. "What would a high powered dealer like that do to an ex-cop investigating him?"

Jo stared hard at the dirt beneath her. When she finally looked up her expression was grave.

"I don't understand how I keep ending up in the middle of your messes, Samantha. Will you ever learn to not be so nosy?"

Samantha swallowed hard. Jo's words hit home. She was the reason that any of them were involved in this.

"I'm sorry," she said quietly. "But it's too late now."

Jo sighed and dusted off her gloves. She tugged one off and then the other. She turned to face Samantha reluctantly. "What do you need me to do?"

"Just a simple break-in. The garden shed is where Jacob would store most of his personal items. I thought maybe he had some work shoes in there that might match the footprints we found. Or maybe even something else that implicates him. We can't search his house, that would be going too far. But if he committed the crime here then there might be something that implicates him in the crime here, too, don't you think?" Samantha looked at Jo with some hesitation. She wasn't sure if Jo would agree, or even if she should.

"All right, a garden shed, that's it. Then I'm done with all of this, understand?" She held Samantha's gaze.

"I understand." Samantha nodded.

***

On the walk to the garden shed Samantha explained to Jo what type of shoes they were looking for and that they weren't very big as the gardener shared the shed with Jacob and Samantha didn't want her to pick up the wrong shoes.

When Samantha and Jo arrived at the garden shed, Walt and Eddy were already there.

"What's this? A reunion?" Jo asked. Her tone was mildly sarcastic.

Eddy offered her a wry smile. Walt only sunk his hands into his pockets.

"We're all here to look out for you, Jo, that's all." Samantha shrugged.

Jo raised an eyebrow. Her expression was one of disbelief, but she didn't protest. "So, what exactly is the plan?" Jo asked.

"We want you to break into the shed and see if Jacob's shoes are in there. They might match the footprints that we found behind my villa and by Vince's body. Can you do it?" Samantha looked at her nervously.

"Of course I can." Jo swept her hair up into a tight ponytail at the back of her neck. Then she walked over to the shed. She glanced over her shoulder at Eddy and Walt. "No watching."

Eddy and Walt glanced at each other. Then they both looked at Jo strangely.

"Why not?" Eddy asked.

"Because I would prefer if you act casual and keep a lookout in case someone is coming as opposed to drawing attention to me breaking into the shed." She eyed them both sternly.

"Look, we don't have a lot of time," Samantha said sharply. "Just do what she asks, please."

Eddy looked at Samantha as if he might argue with her. When she narrowed her eyes he pressed his lips together. "Fine." He hit Walt lightly on his arm, then turned away from the shed. Walt nodded and turned his back to the shed as well. Jo waited until she was sure that they weren't looking. Then she walked around behind the shed. There were no windows, and the front door was too exposed to enter through. She needed to find an alternate entrance.

Jo found a loose seam in the metal shed. She frowned. Climbing through a window or breaking through a lock would be easier than prying open the metal. But it was what she had to do. She reached into her back pocket and pulled out what looked like a thin, metal rectangle. It was made of incredibly strong material. Jo used it to loosen the rest of the metal. Then she eased the metal away. If she pulled it too far she knew that the whole shed would collapse. That would not be very stealthy. She pulled it apart just enough to slip through. The shed snapped closed behind her.

Jo could hear Samantha talking quietly with Eddy and Walt outside the shed. It was good that they were keeping up appearances so that no one would wonder why there was a bunch of people standing around the garden shed. Jo slid the metal rectangle back into her pocket and pulled out a penlight. She used it to look around inside the dim shed. There were plenty of tools, garden supplies, and even a few old tires. She was about to give up looking for the shoes, when she saw a pair tucked behind a large wheelbarrow.

Jo crouched down to get a closer look. They were very worn and caked with dirt. Jo picked them up and grimaced. Not only were they filthy, but they carried a horrid smell. She recognized it as the scent that shoes took on when they had been immersed in water. She did her best not to breathe in the scent and made her way back out of the garden shed. The break-in had gone smoothly, but she still regretted ever having to smell those shoes.

Jo stepped around the side of the shed with the shoes dangling from her fingers. Eddy, Samantha, and Walt were all eagerly waiting for her. Jo refrained from pointing out that their attention was a sure way to get them all caught. "This, is very beneath me." She scrunched up her nose at having to touch the cruddy shoes.

"Sorry it isn't a prettier crime," Eddy quipped.

Jo pursed her lips and handed the shoes to Samantha. Eddy compared the sole of the shoe to the photographs of the footprints on his phone.

"It looks like a perfect match." Eddy offered the phone to Walt so that he could double check. Walt's attention to detail would catch even the smallest difference. When Samantha offered the shoe to him, Walt recoiled.

"I don't have to touch it to look at it. I don't have to smell it either." He pinched his nose as he studied the shoes.

"Yes, everything matches, it seems." Walt nodded. His voice sounded strange with his nose pinched.

"There we go, now we have our proof," Samantha said proudly.

"But not enough to involve the police." Eddy

frowned. "We still can't connect Jacob directly to the murder. I think we're going to need a confession to do that."

"How are you going to manage that?" Jo asked.

"Like I said, we can set a trap." Samantha smiled. "I think it's the best way to get this taken care of quickly."

"It could get messy." Walt frowned.

"Maybe. But I think if Eddy and I are the ones executing it, it will be fine," Samantha nodded with confidence.

"I don't think so." Eddy laughed. "You're not going to be there."

"Yes, I am." Samantha looked at him sternly. "It was my idea."

"That doesn't mean that you can put yourself in danger on my watch, Samantha." Eddy narrowed his eyes.

"Oh yes, Samantha. Don't forget, women must never be daring." Jo rolled her eyes.

"Don't start that, this is not a women's lib thing," Eddy growled.

"Well, it doesn't matter what it is," Samantha declared. "I am going to be there. So, we can either work together, or we can just both be there waiting to get in each other's way."

"Fine. Fine!" Eddy threw his hands in the air. "We can call it a party."

"Don't be difficult." Samantha grinned.

"I'm not getting involved." Walt turned and walked away from the group. Samantha couldn't blame him, with all of the arguing things seemed very chaotic. She knew that Eddy meant well but she wished he would get it through his head that she was capable of investigating crime.

"I'm not getting in the middle of this either," Jo stated. "I promised to break into a garden shed. My job is done." She glanced sympathetically at Samantha and then walked off towards her villa.

Eddy sighed and looked at Samantha. "I guess that just leaves us."

"I guess so," Samantha agreed. "We should have Bill speak about going out tonight in front of Jacob. Then we can hide out in Bill's villa and wait for Jacob to show."

"And what if he shows up with guns or other guys?" Eddy asked.

"We'll just have to figure it out as we go," Samantha suggested. "I'm quick on my feet."

Eddy didn't look pleased, but he reluctantly nodded. He knew a good plan when he heard one.

Chapter Sixteen

That night after Bill had placed the bait by speaking about dinner plans in front of Jacob, Samantha and Eddy slipped into his villa through the back door. Eddy locked it behind them.

"I just want to go on record that I don't agree with you being here," Eddy said.

"You can go on record all you want." Samantha rolled her eyes. "Eddy, you know I can do this. You think you're being protective, but really you're just insulting me."

Eddy paused and turned to look at her. "I didn't realize you took it that way. I'm sorry, Sam."

"Thank you." She felt a little better, but she could still tell that he was uneasy with her being there.

"Let's get in position," Eddy suggested. "I think you should be behind the kitchen island. I'm going to get down behind the couch so that I am close to the table. Please Samantha, if he comes in, let me take care of it. Okay?"

Samantha grimaced and nodded. She felt Eddy was better prepared to handle a physical altercation. She got down behind the kitchen island and watched the door. Then the waiting began. Waiting that seemed like forever. After some time had passed, Samantha whispered to Eddy, "Maybe he's not going to show."

"He'll show. He wants that money," Eddy whispered back.

"But what if he doesn't?" Samantha fretted. "Then all of this will have been for nothing."

"Quiet," Eddy said in a sharp voice. "I hear someone coming."

Samantha nodded. She couldn't see much from behind the kitchen island, but she could hear the footsteps approaching the front door. She held her breath as she heard a key slide into the lock. It was either Jacob using the key from the office, or Bill coming back for something. Samantha's heart began to pound as she heard the door push open. Eddy looked over at her from the couch where he was crouched. Samantha met his eyes briefly and nodded.

A figure walked through the shadows in the living room. It walked right up to the table beneath the attic access. When he started to climb up on top of it, Eddy moved silently forward from behind the couch. In the same moment that the figure pushed the attic entrance open, Eddy tackled him from behind. Samantha stayed down as she had been instructed. She could hear the scuffle of the two men struggling. When she peeked around the edge of the island, she saw that Eddy had Jacob pinned down against the floor. Then Eddy spoke.

"What are you doing in here?"

"I could ask the same about you!" Jacob's voice carried through the villa.

"Bill gave me permission to be here," Eddy growled. "I doubt he gave you permission to be here."

"I don't need permission, I work here," Jacob

shot back.

"That gives you the right to enter a resident's home without permission in the middle of the evening?" Eddy asked. "What are you doing here, Jacob, really?" He twisted the man's arm behind his back until it was painful enough for Jacob to cry out.

There wasn't much that Jacob could do to get out of the hold that Eddy had put him in. Eddy left him enough leeway to lift his head to breathe and speak, but he kept his grip firm. He straddled Jacob's back on one knee with the other foot firmly planted.

"What did you do, Jacob?" Eddy growled.

"Vince was your friend!" Samantha added. She felt secure enough to move out from behind the kitchen island.

"You guys are crazy. Let me go right now!" Jacob squirmed in Eddy's grasp. Eddy pushed Jacob's arm up further along his back. Jacob shrieked in pain and then fell quiet. Jacob grew very still. Samantha was stunned by how strong

Eddy was. To look at him he didn't seem very intimidating, but it was obvious that he had kept in shape over the years.

"We know you were involved in Vince's death." Samantha locked eyes with Jacob. His eyes were wide as he tried to gulp down every trace of air that he could. "Why else would you be here?" Samantha asked.

"Look, I don't know what you two have gotten into your heads, but it's not true. I'm here because I left something in the attic up there." He gritted his teeth.

"Oh, three bags of money?" Eddy asked. "That's not up there anymore."

Jacob pushed his forehead down against the carpeted floor. Eddy ensured that his control over Jacob was still in place. Jacob shuddered in his grip. "You took it?" Jacob asked.

"What we want to know is why did you kill Vince? Wasn't he your friend, Jacob? Isn't he the one who got you this job?" Samantha asked firmly. "Murder doesn't seem like a good way to pay him back."

"He deserved more than that," Jacob bit out each word in a hateful tone. "I could have forgiven him once, he took some money from me to settle his girlfriend's debt. We settled that, and I warned him, if he ever stole from me again he was going to pay the price."

"So, he was stealing the money you were earning from selling illegal drugs?" Eddy asked. "Are we supposed to feel some kind of sympathy about a criminal being double crossed?"

"I loved Vince." Jacob's expression grew solemn. "I loved him like he was my own brother. But he wouldn't stop stealing from me. If I didn't get rid of him, then my boss would have gotten rid of both of us. What was I supposed to do? I warned him, he didn't listen. Was I supposed to die, too?"

Samantha swallowed back her opinion about that. She had researched many crimes over the years. She had found that the ones that involved drugs could be the most ruthless. It churned her stomach to think that a friendship could be turned into homicide over some white powder.

"I think it's time we call in the police," Samantha said quietly. She had gotten caught up in the excitement of the sting and catching a criminal. It seemed like an adventure. However, Jacob's confession had brought her back to reality. She had lost sight of what they were really doing. They had caught a murderer, and even though he would go to prison for his crime, that wouldn't clean up the blood that had been spilled.

"Go ahead and call the police. I'm not afraid. You have no evidence against me. It's just a couple of old feeble memories against me. Who is going to believe you over me?" Jacob laughed a little, but Samantha could see the panic in his eyes.

Eddy chuckled. "Oh, it's much more than that, Jacob. It's those times you got busted for dealing drugs with Vince's brother, Carl. It's your work shoes that match the footprints at the crime scene. Not to mention the bags of money we found in the attic with your fingerprints all over them.

So, it'll be our word against a drug dealer, Jacob. Who do you think they will believe?" He released Jacob and took a step back from him. "You have two choices, Jacob, you can let this go to trial, or you can turn yourself in tonight. If you offer up some information about your drug connections I'm sure that you'll be able to cut a deal. If you let it go to trial, well, I don't know how kindly a jury is going to look upon someone who was willing to murder his best friend. What do you think?"

Jacob looked from Eddy to Samantha and back again. It was clear that he was trying to decide whether to run or not. Samantha knew that wasn't an option. Eddy had his exit blocked.

"There's no escape, Jacob. It's time to pay the price for what you did," Eddy said.

"I didn't have a choice!" Jacob shouted. "He was like a brother to me, but it was him or me. What could I do?"

"You could have gone to the police. You could have done anything other than take the life of someone who trusted you." Samantha glared at him. "Vince was only stealing that money to try to protect someone that he cared about. It doesn't seem right that he had to die for it"

"It's not my fault," Jacob muttered.

"Who was that man you were with last night?" Samantha asked.

"He was an enforcer. He was there to make sure that I had the money and that Vince had been handled. If one thing had been wrong he would have killed me without the slightest hesitation. These are the people I'm dealing with," he spoke anxiously. "I didn't have a choice."

"You made the choice when you began dealing with people like this." Eddy looked at him with some disgust. "You took that risk by getting involved in illegal behavior, and now your friend is dead because of it. Now, you're a murderer, because of it."

Jacob could no longer speak. His expression had gone cold. He stared emptily into the space in front of him. Samantha had seen that look before. It was a look of defeat, Jacob had broken. He wasn't going to fight any more.

"Go ahead and call Detective Brunner," Samantha said.

Eddy pulled out his phone and dialed the detective's number. Detective Brunner answered just before Eddy was about to give up and hang up.

"Eddy, how are interfering in the case now?" he asked.

"It's a good thing I am interfering in your case," Eddy replied. "Why don't you come out to Sage Gardens and pick up the real murderer?"

"Excuse me?"

"I said, we have the right suspect here waiting for you." Eddy frowned.

"We already have a suspect in jail," Detective Brunner sounded argumentative.

"I think that you need to wise up. I just said I have the actual killer here. Get a car out here if you're too lazy to come out yourself," Eddy's voice had raised slightly. It was plain to see that he was fed up with Detective Brunner.

"All right, all right. I'll come right over."

"You do that." Eddy hung up the phone. As he turned to look at Samantha he could see the strain in her expression. Despite the fact that the man standing before her was a confessed murderer, she had sympathy for him. Eddy found that fascinating about her.

"We're going to have to turn over the money, too," Eddy pointed out. "I'll give Walt a call and let him know to get it ready."

Samantha flinched at the mention of the money. She was still the only one that knew that there was money missing from the bags that they had found. She had been putting off the decision about whether to reveal this fact to Eddy or Walt. Now she had to make a choice. Was she going to turn on Jo when their friendship was just starting to strengthen? She met Eddy's eyes. She knew that if she didn't tell him the truth and he found out about it later, he would not forgive her easily. She felt stuck in a bad position. She valued Eddy's friendship, as well as Walt's. But when it came to her friendship with Jo, it wasn't just about herself, it was about Jo, too.

Samantha was fairly certain that she was the only friend Jo had made in a very long time. Samantha could only imagine the devastation that Jo might feel if she finally began to trust someone and was betrayed. Eddy held her gaze for a long moment. Too long. She looked away quickly and focused on Jacob again. He still looked very dazed.

"The more you help the prosecutors the more leniency you'll get," Samantha said. He was a murderer, but the way he looked made her feel a bit sorry for him.

Eddy dialed Walt's phone number, but his gaze lingered on Samantha. He had been sensing it for some time, but now he was sure of it. She was hiding something from him. He didn't know why she would. He thought he had given her every reason to trust him. But apparently it hadn't been enough. Now he was going to have to figure out what it was. He couldn't just ignore it. He needed to know. He could only hope that it wasn't something he didn't want to find out. Eddy was a little startled when Walt answered the phone as he had been lost in thought.

"Hi Eddy, how did it go?" Walt asked.

"It's still going. We're waiting for the police to arrive to take Jacob into custody. I just wanted to make sure that the money was ready."

"Uh, yes, it is," Walt's voice wavered slightly.

"Good, we're going to need to turn it into the police."

"Okay, just meet me over here, I'm not walking anywhere with this much cash."

"No problem. I'll come to get it."

Samantha's heart sank. She knew that time was running out to tell the truth. As Eddy hung up the phone she turned back to look at him.

"Eddy, I need to tell you something."

"I thought you might." He settled his gaze on hers. "What is it?"

Samantha opened her mouth to speak, but before she could, the front door of Bill's villa opened. Detective Brunner walked in with an annoyed frown. "Now, what is all of this about?" he asked.

"Why don't you tell him, Jacob?" Eddy asked. He looked over at the man who had started to tremble a little.

"I want a deal," Jacob spoke in a flat, determined tone.

"A deal for what?" Detective Brunner laughed.

"I want protection. I want a reduced sentence," Jacob insisted.

"Are you offering a confession?" Detective Brunner asked. Now his tone was very stern and interested.

"Yes, and information about one of the largest drug dealers in this city." Jacob cleared his throat. "But I'm going to need protection."

"Well, why don't we just go down to the

station and discuss that?" Detective Brunner suggested. He grabbed Jacob firmly by the arm and began to read him his rights. As Samantha stood back and watched, the two officers that had first investigated the missing backpack stepped into the villa. They cuffed Jacob and led him out of the villa.

Detective Brunner turned to Eddy. "I don't know how you did it, but good work." He shook his head with admiration.

"I'll tell you how I did it." Eddy narrowed his eyes as he looked at the younger detective. "I made sure that I paid attention. I didn't play any games on my phone. I didn't settle for the easiest suspect."

"All right, I see what you're saying." Detective Brunner nodded solemnly. "I guess I still have some things to learn. Maybe you could mentor me a little?"

"Are you serious?" Eddy asked. He raised an eyebrow and scrutinized the detective. Samantha smiled to herself. Compliments always made

Eddy suspicious.

"Yes, I am. I mean, I know it's a lot to ask. But I would love the chance to pick your brain. You're one of the most well-known detectives on the force. Don't you know that?" Detective Brunner smiled.

Eddy looked at him with disbelief. "No, I don't know that. I'm just an old retired cop."

"You're more than that, Eddy. You're John 'Eddy' Edwards. You're a legend. Why do you think everyone is always willing to help you out with whatever you ask?" He looked over at Samantha. "They still tell stories about this man as a rookie."

"Really?" Samantha stepped closer to the two. "I'd love to hear some sometime."

"No, none of that." Eddy shook his head. "What I decide to tell you will have to do."

Samantha held back a laugh at the look of panic in Eddy's eyes. That made her even more curious. However, her amusement faded when

Eddy cleared his throat.

"I need to turn in some other evidence as well."

"Oh? What?" Detective Brunner asked.

"Wait, Eddy." Samantha grabbed his arm.

Detective Brunner looked from Eddy to Samantha. "I'll give you two a minute." He turned and stepped out of the villa to interview Bill who had just arrived.

"What is it, Samantha?" Eddy asked. He studied her intently. "What is it that you're not telling me?"

"I just think maybe we should check in with Walt before we turn in the money," Samantha tried to speak calmly as she knew that her response would only make Eddy more frustrated.

"What can't you tell me now that you can tell me in front of Walt?" he asked. "What's going on here?"

"Please, Eddy. Can we just wait until we have a chance to meet with Walt and get the money from him? I would just feel more comfortable if we did." Samantha braced herself for Eddy's temper. She had noticed that when he felt like he was being lied to or conned he could get pretty angry pretty fast. Instead of shouting though, he only continued to stare at her with a hard expression.

"Fine." He nodded. "I'll go to Walt's first. But that money is getting turned in as soon as possible."

Samantha sighed with relief. She was glad that she had bought herself a few more minutes. She was afraid that if she told Eddy the truth while Detective Brunner was there, that Eddy would insist on having Jo arrested. Samantha definitely didn't want that to happen. However, she wasn't sure how she was going to keep it from happening.

Chapter Seventeen

"Let's go over to Walt's and get the money now." Eddy tilted his head towards the door. He offered Samantha his arm. Samantha hesitated. Eddy noticed the hesitation and shook his head. "I don't know what's going on, Samantha, but I would like to find out. Let's go." He turned towards the door. Samantha followed after him.

They walked in silence towards Walt's villa. With every step Samantha wondered if she was doing the right thing. Would Jo ever be able to forgive her? Would she be able to convince Eddy not to turn Jo in? With so much going on in her mind, she barely noticed that Eddy's expression was stony. When they reached Walt's villa, Walt was waiting at the door.

"Come in." He held the door for both of them.

Eddy remained close to Samantha as they stepped inside. Walt had placed the bags of money on a table which he had covered in plastic wrap in the middle of his kitchen. There were towels on the floor surrounding the table to keep the floor from getting dust on it. Samantha swallowed hard when she saw the bags. She knew that they were light by a few thousand. Would the police know? She guessed that each bag was divided to have an even amount of money, so she guessed that when the police counted it they would wonder where the missing money was. But maybe Jo would be able to get away with it. It's not like criminals kept good accounting records.

"How did it go?" Walt asked. He looked nervously from Eddy to Samantha. It was clear that there was tension between the two of them.

"It went better than expected," Eddy said. He finally looked away from Samantha and towards Walt. "Jacob has agreed to testify about everything, the drugs, the dealers, the money."

Samantha's breath caught in her chest. She realized that when Jacob told the truth about the drugs and the money he would likely share the amount of cash that was in the bags. He also knew that Samantha and Eddy had it in their possession for some time before turning it into the police. When the police went looking for the missing money, they would go right to Samantha and Eddy. Eddy would find out the truth, and Samantha was sure that he would suspect Jo right away. Either way he was going to find out what Jo had done, and that Samantha was hiding it.

"Oh, that's good. That's good. Well then, I guess we better get this money to them." Walt passed a glance over to Samantha. From the look in his eyes Samantha suspected that he knew something as well.

"Not just yet," Samantha said quietly. She refused to look directly at Eddy.

"Samantha, that's it. I want to know what's going on here. Why don't you want to turn in the money?" Eddy's tone was demanding as he stepped closer to her.

"Eddy, I just need a few minutes." Samantha frowned as she pulled out her phone. She was going to see if she could get Jo to bring the money back. That wouldn't exactly solve everything, but it would make things easier.

"A few minutes for what?" Eddy asked. His voice was slightly raised. He was getting more frustrated by the moment. Samantha knew that if she didn't tell him what he wanted to know soon he might just turn in the money without waiting for her. She frowned when she got no answer on Jo's cell phone. She tucked her phone back into her purse.

"Eddy, hear me out before you react," Samantha pleaded.

"Just tell me." Eddy scowled impatiently. Samantha nodded. She prepared herself for his temper.

Eddy looked up swiftly as the door to the villa swung open. Samantha could see the tension in his face as he looked towards the door. Jo stepped inside. She looked at the three with a faint frown.

"Hello."

"Hello yourself." Eddy looked at her with

disbelief. "What's going on?"

"Look, I know that all of this was done to solve a murder. I don't know what's happening to me as the years go by, but I just can't seem to justify profiting from someone's death." She looked crestfallen as she dropped a stack of money in the middle of the table between them. "It's all there."

"What's that?" Eddy asked.

"You're doing the right thing, Jo." Samantha smiled proudly at her.

"You knew about this?" Eddy glanced over at her.

Samantha raised an eyebrow. She looked back at Jo. "I can't say I didn't think about doing the same thing. I mean, who is it really going to hurt to take a little cash?"

"It's a crime for one," Eddy growled.

"It's a financial crime, too," Walt added with a slight shake of his head.

"Which is why I'm giving it back. I don't want anything to do with that life anymore. Taking the money was something I would have done in the past. I don't need it." She eyed the stack with some regret, then turned towards the door. Eddy watched as she walked away. He studied her with a deeper sense of respect. It was one thing to claim that you had changed your life, it was quite another to actually do it.

"Wait! Jo!" Samantha chased after her before she could get out the door. "We're having a drink to celebrate after everything is settled. Would you like to join us?"

Jo glanced over at the two men and shook her head slightly. "I don't think I should."

"Oh, don't worry about them." Samantha waved her hand dismissively. "They're just too old to have any fun."

"Hey!" Eddy scowled at Samantha. "That's not true at all. I can be fun."

"And really, we're probably some of the youngest residents here, Samantha," Walt frowned.

Samantha grinned at their reactions. "See? They need us to loosen them up a bit."

Jo looked over at the two men again. Her gaze lingered on Eddy. There was still quite a bit of friction between them, since her past was in conflict with his.

"If you really want to let go of the past, Jo, then why not start living in the present? With friends?" Samantha offered a hopeful smile.

"Maybe." Jo nodded. With that she turned and walked out of the villa. When the door closed behind her, Walt exhaled.

"She's a tough one, isn't she?" Walt asked. He carefully placed the stack of cash into one of the bags of money.

"She's not so tough. I think she just needs to know what it's like to have friends to rely on." Samantha looked wistfully out the window as she recalled what she knew about Jo's past. The woman had been a loner all her life.

"She has helped us out an awful lot." Eddy

rubbed the back of his neck. "And we haven't exactly shown our gratitude."

"No, we haven't," Walt agreed. "We've behaved rather shamefully."

Samantha was surprised that they seemed to be softening towards Jo.

"I think if we take the time to get to know her, that you will both end up admiring her for who she is. We've all done things in the past that we regret. So, why don't we just give her a real chance?" Samantha remarked.

"Sounds good." Eddy nodded.

"I suppose it's worth a shot." Walt shrugged. "But I'm not letting her near my wallet."

Eddy laughed at that. "Trust me Walt, she does not have any interest in your wallet."

"What? Why not?" Walt frowned. "Is there something wrong with it?"

As the two men debated the value of Walt's wallet, Samantha smiled to herself. Maybe they hadn't been able to prevent a murder, but they had solved it.

Chapter Eighteen

Once the money had been turned in and statements had been taken, Samantha, Eddy, Walt, and Jo met up at a local bar. The hole in the wall bar was not too crowded as the first wave of drinkers had already left. Samantha settled herself at the end of the bar. Jo sat down beside her. Eddy beat Walt to the stool next to Jo. Walt whipped out a wipe from his pocket and polished the seat of the bar stool as well as the bar in front of it before he sat down as well.

"A beer a piece." Eddy nodded to the bartender. Samantha hadn't had a beer in a while, she was looking forward to the frothy taste.

"Could this place be any more seedy?" Jo asked as she glanced around.

"I think that it's quaint." Samantha smiled. "At least we don't have to worry about being bothered by too many people."

"I hope that's the case." Jo smiled as she

accepted her beer from the bartender. The door to the bar opened and Detective Brunner walked in. Samantha recognized him right away. Her stomach knotted. She hadn't expected him. She glanced over at Jo. Would Jo decide to leave if he was there? Or had he come to ask them about why there was a delay in turning in the money?

"Detective!" Eddy waved to the man as he walked towards them.

"Detective?" Jo nearly choked on her beer. Walt reached across Eddy to offer her a napkin. Jo took the napkin and then shot Samantha a look. "Why is there a detective here?"

"I honestly don't know," Samantha kept her voice low as she spoke to Jo. She was just as curious. "I'm sure it's nothing. He probably just wants to speak to Eddy."

"I thought you might like an update." Detective Brunner paused in front of Eddy. Samantha noticed the respectful way he nodded his head to Eddy. Eddy did too. Samantha tried not to chuckle at the proud way he lifted his chin and the smug smile that rose to his lips.

"I'd like that."

"Well, Simon has been released. Jacob admitted that he killed Vince because he had stolen some of the drug money. Vince tried to save himself by throwing the drugs into the water. Jacob followed Samantha and took the backpack back after Samantha found it." Detective Brunner frowned. "A sad story really. But at least it's solved. In fact we will likely get most of the drug ring as a result of Jacob's testimony."

"But what about the screwdriver?" Samantha asked. She still couldn't understand how Simon had the murder weapon when he wasn't the least bit involved.

"Oh, it turns out that Jacob didn't even mean to frame Simon. He panicked and he just hid it the first place he could." He sighed. "When I think of what might have happened to Simon if we hadn't found out the truth about Jacob, it honestly makes me question whether I should be wearing a badge." He lowered his eyes shamefully. "I just can't believe that I made such a mistake."

"Hey, go easy on yourself," Eddy advised. "We all have cases that are close calls. The important thing is that you learn to pay attention and put the work in even when it seems like a slam dunk case. In fact it's usually the ones that seem so simple that end up being something else entirely."

"I know that now, thanks to you," Detective Brunner gratefully acknowledged. "I'm sure I'm going to pick your brain more often when I run into these cases. It's always good to have an experienced set of eyes. I'm sorry for the way that I treated you throughout the case. I'm embarrassed to say that I didn't think you could help in any way. I was a little too caught up in my own ego to recognize that some help could be useful."

"Don't worry about that. I was a cop once. I know what it feels like to be annoyed when someone is interfering with a case. I'm just glad that we were able to help. I'm here to help any time you need it." Eddy smiled and glanced over at his friends. Then he looked back at Detective Brunner. "Join us for a beer?" Eddy offered. He gestured to the bartender to bring another bottle. The bartender walked over and set the bottle down in front of the detective.

"Sure. I'm off duty." Detective Brunner smiled. He seemed relieved that Eddy was so welcoming. It occurred to Samantha that being a detective had to be a rather lonely job. Eddy stood up from his seat and allowed the detective to take it, in a demonstration of respect. Samantha gulped when she saw the detective moving in right beside Jo. She could feel Jo squirming beside her. The detective sat down right next to Jo. Eddy moved over next to Walt. Samantha held her breath for a moment, but she was relieved to see that nothing terrible happened. The bar did not implode. Detective Brunner cast a brief look in Jo's direction, then took a sip of his beer. Jo even smiled as she glanced over at Samantha. Perhaps they were an unlikely group of friends, but Samantha wouldn't change a thing. With them

around, Sage Gardens was a safe place to live once
again.

The End

More Cozy Mysteries by Cindy Bell

Sage Gardens Cozy Mysteries

Birthdays Can Be Deadly

Dune House Cozy Mysteries

Seaside Secrets

Boats and Bad Guys

Treasured History

Hidden Hideaways

Dodgy Dealings

Wendy the Wedding Planner Cozy Mysteries

Matrimony, Money and Murder

Chefs, Ceremonies and Crimes

Knives and Nuptials

Mice, Marriage and Murder

Bekki the Beautician Cozy Mysteries

Hairspray and Homicide

A Dyed Blonde and a Dead Body

Mascara and Murder

Pageant and Poison

Conditioner and a Corpse

Mistletoe, Makeup and Murder

Hairpin, Hair Dryer and Homicide

Blush, a Bride and a Body

Shampoo and a Stiff

Cosmetics, a Cruise and a Killer

Lipstick, a Long Iron and Lifeless

Camping, Concealer and Criminals

Made in United States
North Haven, CT
07 February 2024

48428587R00143